FROM DARKNESS
TO NIGHT

By Michelle D. Jackson

This book is dedicated to my son, Jadin, for his strength and heroism. Loving you has been the greatest gift God has given me.

CONTENTS

From Darkness to Night

Editing by George Fishburne Jr.

This is a work of fiction. Names, characters, businesses, organizations, events, and incidents either are the product of the author's imagination or are used fictiously. Any resemblance to actual persons, living or dead, events, or locales is entirely coincidental.

"Yet the Lord will command His lovingkindness in the daytime, and in the night His song shall be with me, and my prayer unto the God of my life." Psalm 42:8

PART I - DARKNESS

CHAPTER 1: BOILED WATER

2006

J oAnn stood impatiently over the bathroom sink, waiting for the washbasin to fill with water. Her red and swollen eyes were dotting unrelentingly between the running faucet and the white washcloth gripped in the palm of her hand. A single bead of sweat gathered at the corner of her temple, while the tears she'd fought to hold back broke free and cascaded effortlessly down her cherry-tanned cheeks.

Reneata, JoAnn's oldest daughter, lay barely conscious on the cold tile floor with her head just inches from the commode's base. Convinced that if she moved one inch, she would lose the fleeting breath of life that quietly exited her dying body, she lay still, as still and somber as a buried corpse.

"Baby, can you hear me?" JoAnn cried, straddling her knees over Reneata's upper torso. Intentionally pressing her warm body against Reneata's chest, she wiped the damp cloth across her daughter's brow before grabbing her right arm and wrapping a second layer of bandage around the bleeding gash on her wrist.

Reneata could feel the thump of JoAnn's heartbeat against her chest. She'd never felt its splitting rhythm before. Its pounding quake brought a singe of hope into her heart, awakening her, and shining a light on JoAnn, whom Reneata could now see clearly - more clearly than at any other time in her life. Despite their fragile past, at that moment, the woman straddled over her was no longer a stranger. Instead, she was caring and kind, and not the mother who'd struggled to be good to her and her siblings most of their lives.

Intentionally ignoring Reneata's piercing eyes, just as she'd ignored her own image in the bathroom mirror moments before, JoAnn focused solely on wrapping her daughter's arm with the bandage.

JoAnn was hiding, although her daughter was not fooled. Looking into the face of the woman who gave birth to her 24 years ago, Reneata could no longer escape the truth – she loved her mother the only way she knew how, despite her fears that love was never enough.

As calm eased the panic in the room, Reneata felt something wet under her body. Struggling to raise her head for the second time — now less fearful to move than before – she saw a pool of blood next to her bandaged arm and a silver razorblade near her chest. *Oh my God, why did I do this?* she thought. Her fears chased a million things through her mind. But seeing the razor blade on the floor made it clear that she had, indeed, tried to hurt herself.

As painful as it was to accept that she'd surrendered to her most horrid fears, she knew what she'd done could not be reversed. It would change everything – her already unstable relationship with her mother and sister, and the life she'd planned with her fiancé Ty, the man she'd opened her heart to despite her own insecurities and doubts.

Reneata had desperately wanted everyone in C-Way, the neighborhood she grew up in, to believe that she was strong and un-rattled by the mistakes of her past, but now they would know how broken she truly was.

She'd never wanted to hurt herself before that day, but the sight of her beloved brother, Ervin, dead in her mother's bedroom, had been too much to handle. She gave in to the darkness, never expecting JoAnn to be a beacon of light. She was wrong. The universe needed her here. There was more to do.

The blaring sounds of multiple sirens startled JoAnn and

Reneata.

"Don't move," JoAnn cautioned before bolting from the bathroom, heading towards the front door. In a heartsick, whispery voice, she cried out, "Why!" as she ran through the narrow hallway.

After twelve years of watching her family fall apart, Reneata knew her mother wasn't questioning her; she was - without any doubt - questioning God. They had all questioned Him at some point or another. The culmination of their grief had done nothing to change their fate, and the pain of it all was proof that God was not listening.

Two paramedics struggled to get Reneata off the floor of the bathroom. Her long legs could barely bend high enough to allow the paramedics to get a small portion of the gurney in the narrow space. One of the paramedics, a tall, but awfully slender white man, who wouldn't stop calling her name, straddled his thin legs over the commode to better situate her body. Placing a small, sturdy board behind her head, he slid her a few inches from the floor so the other paramedic - a short, dark-skinned black woman with a neat, low-cut fade - could get the gurney partially into the room. Reneata could hear and see everything going on around her, but she couldn't say a word. She didn't cry or groan in pain; she just lay there, watching their quick and sudden movements while praying it would all come to an end.

When the paramedics rolled her onto the gurney and started towards the front door, Reneata caught a glimpse of JoAnn outside the bathroom, crying into the arms of a white police officer. He held her with caution, while instructing the other officers with a nod of his head, to look for evidence. Three cops, including an older Asian man in a suit, started looking through the meager, two-bedroom, one-story bungalow for clues. It was a crime scene, and someone – possibly one of the two living people found in the house – could be held accountable for murder.

In a trembling voice, JoAnn told the officer that Ervin had stumbled to her door just past 10 a.m. that morning, bleeding from his chest, with a large stab wound on his upper thigh. He was scared - appeared to be running from someone - and was begging for her help. In a panic, she swung the screen door open, grabbed her slender 5'10" eldest son by his arm, then dragged him to the bedroom before racing to the kitchen to call 911. But just as she picked up the phone, she heard a car pull into the driveway, and saw a stocky, young black man dressed in blue jeans and a black jacket run towards the house. She admitted that she did not know him, but she could see a gun protruding from his waist and hear the driver tell the man to "find him!" Within seconds, he was in her home, hunting for Ervin.

Terrified, JoAnn hid in the small space between her refrigerator and the wall. She admitted to having 'no courage' and being 'frozen in fear.' A stranger was in her home; her son was badly wounded, and now, because she was unable to protect him, the sound of a single gun-shot rang throughout the house, and she heard what no mother would ever want to hear – her child make his final pleas for help. Seconds after the gun went off, the man ran from the house, jumped into the running car, and spun down the street.

"I did nothing to save my son!" she cried out. The cop – Officer Stewart – who was rightfully shaken by her sobering grief, tried to console her with a sterile pat to her shoulder, but the ache in her voice could not be mended.

As expected, the next question had to do with Reneata. Officer Stewart, whose voice was so smooth that it made everything he said sound like a public service announcement, politely asked JoAnn to explain, to the best of her ability, what had happened to her daughter. Why was her daughter barely conscious and bleeding from a wound to her wrist while on the bathroom floor? How could two siblings be critically injured in JoAnn's home? Who hurt her son and when did her daughter get to the house?

The questions spiraled in the air like a tornado funnel. JoAnn, overtaken by the enormity of it all, took one step away from the officer, then began to collapse to the floor. Catching her by the arms, Officer Stewart picked her up without wavering and carried her limp body to the couch. Then he directed a paramedic, with yet another nod of his head, to come to her aid.

The truth was, JoAnn had no clue why Reneata had shown up at her house that morning. She and her daughter hadn't spoken that day. Reneata had recently moved into her own place, a few blocks away, and JoAnn typically only saw her at Morrison's Bakery, where they both worked a 2 – 10 p.m. shift most days. They'd had no plans to see each other before their shift started. But that didn't stop Reneata from bolting in the door, barefoot, and reeking of booze, just after the gunman and his driver sped down the street. Reneata was screaming Ervin's name; she knew something bad had happened, but JoAnn had no idea how.

After the paramedics broke an ammonia inhalant under JoAnn's nose, she woke, pushed past the policemen, and then ran into the street. Her neighbors crowded the sidewalk, watching as her two oldest children were hauled off in separate ambulances.

Reneata, strapped to a gurney inside one of the ambulances, caught a glimpse of JoAnn before the vehicle's doors were shut. Closing her eyes tightly to pray – something she hadn't done in many years – she knew the time had come, and she was in no place to avoid surrendering.

CHAPTER 2: NO LONGER THE PAST

"He called me 'Sweet Thang,'" Reneata cried out a bit incoherently. The same smooth-talking white cop who had tried consoling JoAnn at the house stood inches from her bed with a small note pad in his hand. He had wasted no time interviewing Reneata as soon as she reached the hospital. Although she was fighting fatigue and hysteria, she garnered the strength to give him details about the accident, and what took place in the hours leading to her arrival at JoAnn's front door.

Officer Stewart, like most of the people in the old neighborhood, knew Reneata and her family well. Ervin was a legend in his own right. A young prodigy, his art and creativity had been closely followed by people across the state of Alabama. Reneata, his younger sister, was valedictorian of her high school class and homecoming queen two years in a row. One of the prettiest and smartest girls in the school, not even her checkered past could blemish her popularity in the small, working-class community.

Struggling to get comfortable, Reneata's body felt limp and disjointed, as if she'd been unwound from a tangled spool of cord. Her head, which felt unusually heavy, was shaken like a baby's rattle. She knew from the cocktail of medicine the paramedics had pumped into her IV while she was inside the ambulance that she wouldn't make it home any time soon, and the awful uneasiness she felt in the core of her stomach was there to stay.

"Sweet Thang, do you hear me!" Reneata yelled at the cop. A nurse came into the room and asked her to keep it down. But Reneata was trembling uncontrollably from the medicine and the overwhelming stress on her tired body.

"Ma'am, what exactly does that mean, 'Sweet Thang'?" the officer asked, while scribbling on the notepad like he was writing a verbatim account of a murder, and she was the only eyewitness to the crime.

"Are you listening?" she cried. "My brother is dead, and I know who did it!"

"Ok," Officer Stewart said after taking a long, deep breath, in hopes she would follow his lead and calm down. "I'm listening. Start from the beginning. How do you know who shot your brother?"

Reneata gathered her composure, wiped the tears from her cheeks, then began to talk. She could hear Gramps say, 'cooperation is the key to surviving the criminal system; if you can't stay out of trouble, do what you can to keep those in power on your side'. She had not understood his words when she was younger, but now, amid a crisis, she needed the police to believe her.

"I'm not sure where to start but I'll do my very best," she said. "This isn't something I've talked about much in the past but if it will help you find Ervin's killer I will tell you everything I know."

Nodding his head in agreement, then pulling a chair from the corner of the room, Officer Stewart sat next to her bed and listened for the next hour as she told him everything she knew, and where to find the murderer.

An hour before Ervin was shot, Reneata had awakened in her bed, in a drunken stupor after a long night of partying with her girls at Savoy's Place, her favorite hole-in-the-wall night club in the city. Only a few days had passed since Ty, her boyfriend for more than three years, proposed marriage, and she was celebrating. Hard. Maybe a little too hard. But they had been through so much together. He was the first man she'd ever truly loved, and the very idea of starting a new life with him and putting some distance between herself, her family, and Alabama made her over-the-top happy.

The week after Ty's proposal, he had shipped off to basic Army training, and left Reneata to get things in order before he returned. They'd made plans to marry at the church her grandfather attended when his basic training was over, then spend the next few years living on military bases and seeing the world. Although he made her promise not to go to Savoy's while he was away, she couldn't resist. She'd been drinking a lot since Ervin was released from prison six months before, and Ty was doing everything he could to keep her out of trouble.

In a weak and melancholy voice, she began to tell Officer Stewart everything she remembered.

"My phone began ringing just past 10:15 a.m. this morning, and it wouldn't stop," she said. "I rolled out of bed and made my way to the kitchen to answer it. When I picked up the receiver, a strange but slightly familiar voice said, 'Re, it's time.' Time for what? I didn't understand at first."

"The man repeated, 'Re. It's time.' The voice was raspy and phony; he sounded like he was playing a game. So, I laughed, thinking it was Ty disguising his voice or one of my other friends. It was so random and strange, and the person knew my nickname, so I didn't think much of it."

"When the phone was completely quiet, I announced that I was hanging up and warned this person not to call again. But just as I removed the phone from my ear, the caller said something that immediately got my attention. He called me "Sweet Thang", then mentioned Ervin's name. That's all it took for me to know that it was Randall, the older brother of Byron, a guy I'd dated many years before."

"I'd waited on that call but hoped it would never come. But once it did, I knew something bad would follow."

The last time Reneata had seen or heard from Byron Lucks

or his brothers, Randall and Leon, was in 1991. She had been fif-
teen-years-old. Byron was her first boyfriend, but after years of
physical abuse and mental manipulation, Reneata realized that
he wasn't a good guy; he was a low-life and a drug dealer, and
she'd given him her innocence and trust for far too long.

Byron and his brothers were known on the streets for
beating down guys and roughing up women. Barely two years
apart in age, by their eighteenth birthdays, each brother had
spent time in at least two juvenile detention centers.

On the streets, their dark past was considered a badge of
honor, a symbol of their manhood, and they wore it like an oversized gold chain with a diamond cross as its centerpiece.

Byron, the middle brother, was a ruthless gang-leader
who had a thing for young girls, and Reneata had been in his
purview since she was twelve-years-old and he was twenty-one.
His broad shoulders, caramel-brown skin, and New York accent
were all he needed to attract most of the girls in the neighborhood, including Reneata. Although she had seemed mature for
her age, she was nothing more than a little girl seeking the safety
and security of someone who cared – a daddy figure - and Byron
represented that. She had Gramps, and she loved him dearly, but
Reneata was a kid in need of guidance. JoAnn was too busy dealing with the flow of worthless men who paraded in and out of
their home most of Reneata's life to notice that her 12-year-old
daughter was getting into trouble. She'd left Reneata and her siblings to live aimlessly, tumbling through life like the seeds of a
wishing flower.

Reneata fell hard for Byron, believing that he would be
there for her, but after years of being with him, selling drugs,
protecting his business in ways too explicit to admit, and bringing shame to her family, she realized that he would never
change.

"Byron grabbed me by the neck one night and choked me
until I was blue in the face. That was the last time I saw him,"

Reneata told the officer. "I wish I could say it was the first time he had hit me, but it wasn't. Things had gotten out of control, but for some reason, that day, I wasn't as afraid to defend myself as I had been in the past, so I fought back...."

"What do you mean?" the officer interrupted when she paused to get her composure.

"He tried to kill me, but I wouldn't let him. I took the tip of my house key and cut him just under his ear."

"Did he retaliate?"

"He tried, but he couldn't," she said, raising her head slightly from the pillow. "Seconds after his hands fell from around my neck, he hit the floor. Unknowingly, I'd pierced an artery in his neck. I could have killed him. His brothers ran into the room, dragged him to the car, but not before threatening me. Randall promised that I would regret what I did. He didn't care that his brother had tried to kill me or that I was only 15-years-old. He didn't care that I was scared to death and too young to even understand what the hell I'd gotten myself into. He only cared about protecting Byron's street-cred."

Officer Stewart stopped writing long enough to focus on a stray tear rolling down Reneata's face. He watched as the tear dripped from her chin onto the hospital gown.

"We had to relocate for a while," she continued. "JoAnn and Gramps were afraid for me. I spent years looking over my shoulders," she paused. "'Sweet Thang' is what Byron and his brothers called me."

"You think it's the Lucks brothers returning to retaliate?"

"Yes. I have no doubt."

When Reneata heard the man on the phone call her 'Sweet Thang', a chilly breeze had run across her face and arms. Despite the high humidity, she'd felt a chill. Something was trying to wake her from her drunkenness, and while she attempted to shake it off, fear swarmed into her mind like bees just before settling in. And that was when it hit her: *O my God, Ervin!*

Twenty strides later, she was in the alley, running the five blocks to JoAnn's house, looking for her brother. Her bare feet traveled as fast as the hot gravel would allow. The sun had no mercy on her hung-over body: cheap liquor poured out of her in tiny beads of sweat that soaked her tank top, and dribbles of saliva crowded the corners of her mouth. Cars stopped in the middle of the road to let her pass, and strangers stood on their porches, as if to usher her along. It was as if they knew what was happening – they'd gotten the same call and had heard the hateful revenge in Randall's voice.

"When I got to JoAnn's, my brother was dead. I couldn't handle it," she said, glaring at her bandaged wrist, then squeezing her eyes together tightly to stop a rush of tears from falling. "It was Byron and his brothers who killed him, and it's my fault."

By the end of her story, Reneata lay exhausted on the flat and uncomfortable hospital bed, waiting for the officer to race from the room and start looking for the Lucks brothers. But instead, the overly polite Officer Stewart nonchalantly closed his notepad, then looked her square in the eyes.

"To clarify, Ms. Morris," he said, in a syrupy-sarcastic tone. "You believe the sibling of an ex-boyfriend of yours from nine years ago, when you were 15, killed your brother as revenge due to an unfortunate incident between you and some asshole drug dealer?"

"Yes!" she insisted.

"Okay.... Well. I will look into it by first confirming if the Lucks brothers were in the city at the time. I remember those guys. They were bad news, but no one has heard from them in years. In the meantime, I want you to get better so you can help us make sense of all of this."

"What do you mean, 'make sense of all of this'? It was

them!" she cried. "I have no doubt! Why would I get the call? There's no other explanation."

"There is," he said, and she met his subtle sarcasm with a harsh roll of her eyes. "What about your brother's drug addiction? He got out of prison weeks ago, right? Three years at the state pen for robbery. He's got enemies."

"And! My brother also has a community of people who loves him. Don't forget who you are talking about. If you know about his time away, then you know about his work."

"I do. The best damn artist this state has seen in years. A prodigy. But that doesn't change what he ultimately became. And what about your mother, JoAnn? She doesn't have a stellar reputation in the community, but you know this."

"No! Ervin was getting better, he was creating again, getting his life together. And JoAnn may be a crummy mother, but she doesn't have enemies. This is about me and my past," Reneata cried. "I just gave you everything you need to catch these assholes, and you're telling me I'm wrong!"

"Okay. Okay. Calm down and get some rest. This is a priority case for us. Regardless of what you think, we respect what your brother accomplished, and understand how his addiction hurt the family and the community. But he was a criminal who chose to surround himself with other criminals, and we can't overlook that fact. However, I promise to investigate your claims and catch this bastard. We will be in touch soon."

Reneata reluctantly shook her head in agreement.

After Officer Stewart left the room, she thought about what he had said and made a promise to herself to do everything she could to help them find her brother's killer.

CHAPTER 3: MAGICAL PEOPLE

Ervin was an artist in every sense of the word. He was always making things – turning cardboard boxes into dollhouses and drawing murals on the wall of his bedroom. It was as if he were a magician wielding a type of magic that his family didn't always understand. While the rest of the boys in the neighborhood learned to master street-wisdom and hood decorum, Ervin was sitting in his room, crafting another piece of art.

A curly-haired, chunky-cheeked black boy with big, light brown eyes, he had just turned 13 when he started molding what looked like mud in his hands and forming odd-looking animals and oblong structures that made no sense to JoAnn and Gramps. But when his creations were completed, hardened, and painted; when every line, every contour had been perfected, it was a work of art.

Like most artists, he grew into his craft. Getting better and better every year. Winning competitions across the state, and spending his summers in art camps taught by world-renowned artists. Reneata had been a young girl at the time, but she understood that something big was happening. She watched in awe as her brother got the attention of people everywhere. People who didn't look like her or her family. People who lived differently than they did.

They were poor. No one said it. No one had to. But their lack was as thick as stacked boulders. JoAnn had given birth to three kids by three different men, and she raised them in a town called Tinsley, outside of Birmingham, Alabama for most of their lives. None of her children knew their father. All they had was Gramps, who cared for them like they were his own.

Tinsley was jammed between the city of Birmingham to

the east and steel plants and racecar complexes to the west. A place filled with plain folks who spoke unsophisticated words that tasted like sweet tea every time they left their lips. Reneata, and her family, were one of them. The magical. The less-ordinaries. The loyal. The Believers. And she was good with that, although JoAnn never was.

C-Way was another name for the 'old neighborhood', although the three-foot-high steel placard at the entrance read: Edward D. Cummings Housing Projects. Side-by-side government-issued brick boxes with two-foot-high cement porches, and close to 90 families who called them *home*. JoAnn's home had a green porch swing and an oversized window AC that groaned far louder than it cooled, and a big oak tree hanging over the side wall, practically to the dividing slab of cement separating her three-bedroom apartment from her neighbor's. Despite a yard covered in toys and playing kids, they lived in peace in a place that the world depicted as sad and poverty-stricken. Thank God, it never felt that way.

Until Reneata was 15-years-old, they lived on the corner of Cummings Circle and Alpine Road. Years before it became the deadliest street in the city, The Circle, as it was called, was *the-place-to-be*. In the center of the neighborhood there was a large patch of concrete – a parking lot – most often covered with kinfolks with no bloodline, instead of cars. Play cousins, uncles, and Buddy James, who had their own families but didn't mind catching wildin' out neighborhood kids by the collars of their shirts and dragging them kicking and screaming to their doorsteps. Play aunties and God mommas who would stop Reneata in the dead of night, chastise her for wearing her skirt too short, then fill her arms with plates of food wrapped in aluminum foil, slices of homemade cake, and ice cold Faygo sodas.

Most nights, The Circle boomed with music flowing from all directions. A generation of hip-hop fiends swayed and hopped, prepped and boogied as if the twinkling moon was a disco-ball, and the city curbs were the outskirts of a packed dance floor. Small packages moved from hand to hand, and money traveled at lightning speed in the darkest corners of the street, but no one paid much attention to that. No one allowed it to disturb the music. They all got their high one way or the other.

All it took was for the hot Alabama sun to go down, and everyone who found their way to The Circle had rhythm. Everyone listened intently for their theme song, then waited as the one guy with the biggest boom box played them off. It was the late 80's, early 90's, and they danced wildly, laughed loudly, and forgot about everything else. A serious drug scene was heating up, but the people in C-Way never thought it would reach them in the Heart of Urban Dixie.

Magical people. That's what Gramps called them. The rent was due, welfare checks went missing from mailboxes, and no-credit-needed furniture filled their homes. To the privileged, they didn't have much, but they had this odd kind of magic that got them through. And that's why C-Way held Reneata's story. It was the best place she knew, filled with the best people God ever created.

Ervin's teachers called him a 'prodigy'; JoAnn simply called him blessed. She had something to be proud of - they all did. He was gifted, and they shared his bloodline.

When Ervin was fifteen, Gramps built a 10 x 10 room on the back of his little house. He cashed in his pension from the coal mine and filled the room with kilns and clay; he decorated the walls with pictures of ceramic art and installed oak shelves to showcase his grandson's work. He was a proud man - a substitute father to a very special boy. Ervin was his son; there was no light of day between them. Ervin would be great. Everyone was certain of it.

But greatness had its expiration date, and Ervin's date came too soon. When he turned nineteen, and Reneata was twelve, he had been on the cusp of leaving Alabama for a prestigious art school in New York. He OD'd on heroin in his bedroom. Reneata remembered the console TV in the front room that had been blasting Jay Leno's *Tonight Show* monologue while the paramedics tried to save her brother. No one thought to turn the volume down or to keep out the prying eyes of the outside world. From the moment of his first transgression, Ervin's addiction was on full display, just like a piece of his most celebrated artwork.

The memories of that night were etched in Reneata's mind. No matter how hard she tried, she could not forget it. She and her little sister, Tess, hid in the closet. Strangers tracked through their house. JoAnn paced the floor, angrily shoving the butt of an unlit cigarette into her mouth. She was screaming at the paramedics. "Do your job! Do it right! You hear me! You better not put that white sheet over my baby's face! I fucking dare you!"

Reneata was sure Ervin was dead. She'd never really thought about death until that night. But after that time, she was often reminded of the many things in this world that are so easily lost.

Heroin ultimately robbed Ervin of his talent, and then he robbed Ms. Quaker, who lived on 5th Street, for her stereo and a broken microwave. He didn't go to art school; he didn't set the world on fire as the family had hoped. Instead, he went to the penitentiary. Twice.

The family had been convinced that Ervin would pull them from the mire of poverty. They were like the Evans Family, straight from the 1970's sitcom *Good Times*. Counting their chickens before they hatched, forgetting how unpredictably harsh the real world could be.

Right before her eyes, Reneata's beautiful and artistic

brother transformed into an ugly, self-loathing drug addict, and criminal. Life just wasn't fair.

CHAPTER 4: GRAMPS

2 Days at Bethany Skylar Institution

The sound of rubber-bottom shoes scratching against the tile floor woke Reneata from her sleep. "Baby girl, what happened? What happened to Ervin?" Gramps said, as soon as she opened her eyes. His beloved grandson was dead, his granddaughter was confined to the worst mental institution in the state, and his daughter, whom they knew all too well had shut down mentally, just as she'd done so many times in the past.

Without raising her body from the sunken mattress, Reneata's eyes dotted from the spackled white ceiling and grubby blue walls to the painful IV needle inserted into her hand. For the first time since being at the hospital, she noticed the wood-framed chair with a torn green cushion in the corner of the room, and an open Bible on a table near the window. Next to the Bible was an empty, fuchsia lipstick-stained cup lying idly on its side. Someone had been there who liked the same shade of lipstick that JoAnn often wore, but Reneata had little doubt it was hers. She knew, once JoAnn heard that Byron may have had something to do with Ervin's death, she would not want to see her.

Gramps's big hands stroked Reneata's hair, and the smell of coal smoke filled the room. After working for thirty years in the coal mines, the smell followed him like a relentless shadow. It was how she knew it was her Gramps - his pride hugged him like a perfectly tailored suit even when he wore nothing but rustic denim overalls and a white T-shirt.

Someone had removed the bandage from around Reneata's right wrist to keep the wound clear of irritation. With her left hand, she tugged at the mouth of Gramps's pocket when he stood over her bed to kiss her on the forehead. From his pocket, Reneata pulled the handkerchief that he always carried. When he saw the gesture, he knew his granddaughter was back. It was something she had often done when she was a little girl, to remind her that he was her one, predictable thing.

Gramps touched her hand when it reached his pocket and gave it a gentle tug. The church deacon in him always knew how to make everyone, even a stranger, feel loved.

"Sweetheart, what happened to you? What happened to Ervin?"

Groggily, Reneata pointed her liberated hand in the direction of the water pitcher, and he quickly grabbed a Styrofoam cup and filled it partially before bringing it to her parched lips for a soothing sip. He was waiting. Impatiently, she must admit. Not that she could blame him.

It only took one glare into Gramps's eyes to know that there were no words to make him understand. So, instead of trying, she eased the handkerchief back into his hand, and then pretended to fall asleep.

Wrestling with what to do next, Gramps eventually pulled the chair with the torn green cushion from the corner, sat as close as he could to her bed, and waited for her to wake again.

The soft, yet potent, texture of his prayers filled every dark space inside the hospital room. The sound of his baritone voice reminded Reneata that she was loved. He sang, almost in a whisper, her favorite song. The one she yearned to hear when she was at her loneliest. Like the nights when she lay cradled in her bedroom and listened as Ervin crooned a song of satisfaction after getting high in the room next door. The thump of his frail body against the floor when the high got so good, it rocked him to sleep. Or the many days when she and her sister Tess were left in the house alone for hours at a time while Gramps and JoAnn searched the streets for Ervin. He would go missing for days, stumbling through back alleys, sleeping inside shambled sheds in a stranger's backyard. When he returned to them, at the height of his addiction, there would be so little that resembled the brother they loved. He'd changed from a strong, creative soul, to skin, bones, and desperation.

The song Gramps sang reminded her of Jesus's love, despite what she felt inside. It gave her hope, the one thing she needed most.

Gramps knew that although Reneata hadn't stepped foot inside a church in over five years, that she needed reminding of God's love. He brought with him the presence of a good God that no one in her life, before or after that day, ever could.

An hour passed, and Reneata had not moved nor said a word. Somewhere between pretending and wrapping herself in the comfort of Gramps's presence, she almost fell asleep. When he realized that she wouldn't open her eyes any time soon, he gathered his cap, kissed her on the forehead, and headed toward the door.

When the door slid partially shut behind him, Reneata pulled the covers from over her face and listened to the one man she'd loved her entire life, lean against the door and weep. There was something about a grown man crying that reminded her of the coldness of this world. All she wanted to do was protect him from the ugliness of her past and lighten the burdens he bore over their family's fate.

She remembered Gramps walking with her, hand in hand, to the neighborhood playground to hunt for four-leaf clovers in the grass when she was a little girl. While they waddled around on their knees, he would tell her stories about the beautiful places he wanted her to see when she grew up. Gramps had never traveled, rarely left the state where he had raised JoAnn, but he was an avid reader and a wonderful storyteller who wanted his three grandkids to live a better life than he had lived.

He called Reneata a 'rambler' because, even as a young girl, she was in search of many things. Whether it was his handkerchief, four-leaf clovers in the grass, or pebbles in a sandbox, he loved that she was an adventurer, and wanted nothing less for his eldest granddaughter than a life of discovery.

By the time Reneata was ten, Gramps had taken her to every corner of the globe with his make-believe stories about a little girl, a 'rambler', who'd touched the tamped earth of the Great Wall of China and washed her hair in the Nile River. He told her that she would one day see all the beauty God had made. Reneata believed him, although she'd had no clue how to make her dreams come true until she met and fell in love with Ty.

Getting from where she was, lying in that hospital bed, to where she wanted to be – where Gramps wanted her to be – seemed impossible. All her dreams, all her goals, her love for a good man, were pointless now. She had disappointed everyone, but nothing hurt her more than disappointing the man who prayed for her as vehemently as her grandfather did.

Gramps was born Sigmund Ervin Tate, but no one called him by that name. He was Gramps to everyone, which was ironic because he never looked a day over fifty. One generation removed from the bowels of Black Seminoles, and two generations from slavery. His native blood ran deep - christening him with the most polished brown skin and jet black, silky hair. He looked like something mystic, untold, and rare. Like an antique book filled with the most beautiful illustrations, or a one-hundred-year-old copper coin.

"The last southern gentleman," Mill, JoAnn's neighbor and best friend from C-Way, would say between rocking one baby on her hip and screaming at the other three. JoAnn struggled to give her friend a squint of agreement, not that she couldn't recognize how special Gramps was: a single black man, still relatively young, untarnished by the dirt and heat of the coal mines he had toiled in most of his adult life, and seemingly unfazed by the responsibility of raising a young girl alone.

Gramps was all the family Reneata knew, besides JoAnn and her siblings. Although, he had a twin brother – Uncle Toot, whom no one said much about. He died when Reneata was in the fourth grade. The first and only time she saw his face was the day of his funeral. A day that always stuck in her mind because it was the first time she saw JoAnn cry.

Reneata wasn't sure if her real Grandma – Contessa Tate – had been white or Indian or just a light-skinned black lady. The story was, Gramps met her somewhere near New Orleans, off the bay of the lake with the funny name. He'd left Florida, looking for a better life. It was the 1950's. She was thirteen and alone, wandering the streets in search of food. Her family, Reneata's great-grandparents, had perished in a fire in a nearby town, and nobody wanted her. Gramps took her in, never caring about her race or the danger a young black man could find himself in while cavorting through the Deep South with a young girl who wasn't his wife. But they survived, somehow, took root in Alabama, and had a child.

Reneata's grandma died when JoAnn was two, after surviving the loss of her family and clinching relentlessly to the handsome man with legs so long she spent nights altering his work pants to keep the holes in his socks from showing. Contessa died in her sleep. She was barely twenty-years-old. The sum of her life was a closet filled with hand-stitched work pants, a daughter who would never know her, and a picture. JoAnn had the original, and Gramps kept a faded copy nailed to the wall in his tiny front room.

Reneata often stood staring at her grandmother's picture, searching for resemblances of herself to her family, making up stories of who she was or who she wanted her to be. She grieved the way a granddaughter could, although no one spoke Contessa's name or gave heart to anything memorable about her life. She was an enigma, unintentionally watching over them from a very distant place. Regretfully, Reneata imagined, not leaving more of herself to pass along to her grandkids.

In Reneata's dreams, her grandmother was glamorous, like Dorothy Dandridge and Lena Horne. No doubt, she could have been an actress. Grandma Tess had been beautiful. Flawless. Her skin was light. Her hair, long and curly. She was short but shapely, and absolutely stunning. Her photo gave her family the only opportunity to know her, and to look into her eyes. JoAnn looked so much like her mother, but she looked nothing like most of the black folks in the old neighborhood.

Despite her flaws, JoAnn was an exceptionally beautiful black woman. Her skin was like the inside of a sliver of almond. Her hair, thick, jet black, and wavy. Back in the 80's and early 90's she had worn it meticulously pulled into a bun and tucked behind her left ear. Reneata would watch her mother through the crack in her bedroom door almost every night before bed, as she would let her hair down. It hung to the creases of her elbows.

JoAnn was petite but curvy, and wonderfully made, as their mailman, Rob, would often proclaim. She was the ending to the sentence, 'so she pretty like…' that other women hated to hear a man say. She had a peculiar realness that didn't belong in the old neighborhood. Homecoming queen. Most popular. Most doable. Most wanted, but more importantly, most needed.

She was radiant like the sun, for a while. Reneata wanted to be her. She idolized the way men glared without blinking. The way women spoke about her in kindness with one side of their mouths, and despised her with the other side. She loved how JoAnn knew she was beautiful, but never had to say it out aloud or proclaim it to the world in any way. She was just who she was. And being broke didn't change it; having three kids didn't change it. Her beauty was hers to do with as she pleased, and without any doubt, it was used to get the things she wanted.

JoAnn was the type of momma who would spank her children six hours later for something they had done to disrupt her soap opera, or for not speaking to a houseguest the very moment they entered the room. Just as the children tried to explain their intentions, they would find themselves in a round of lashes.

JoAnn chain-smoked cigarettes. Her well-manicured fingers were wrapped around a Newport more often than around the shoulders of her kids.

She was loud and funny. Street smart and unforgiving. Although she was traditionally beautiful – light skin with long hair – she was unconventionally witty and charismatic.

But like most attractive things, JoAnn's beauty was fleeting. Held up by faulty ground and mistaken for confidence.

Reneata learned about her mother's unkind ways, at ten-years-old, when JoAnn forgot her birthday. Left her sitting at the bus stop, draped in a birthday hat, holding the remains of a cake she'd shared with her classmates after Gramps surprised her in class with a party. JoAnn never came. She said she had something better to do, reassured Reneata she'd have other birthdays, then yelled at Gramps for getting off work on her daughter's behalf.

Reneata was ten-years-old, and her momma didn't want to be with her on her birthday. That was when she became 'JoAnn', to her little girl. Although Reneata continued to call her momma until the day she graduated high school, it was at the age of ten when she started struggling to see JoAnn as a loving, kind, nurturing woman.

For years, Reneata blamed grandmomma Contessa's death for what happened to JoAnn. Who could be happy with no momma around? There was only so much Gramps could do alone. Kids could survive without their daddies, but mommas were like the air they breathed.

The darkness got in. Flushed away better times long before Ervin got sick. He was the jewel in her crown when at his best – making art, proving to the world that she had given birth to a genius. But when his talent was no longer revered, Ervin became the nail in her coffin.

CHAPTER 5: SIS

Day 5 at Bethany Skylar

"Ain't that bad, is it, Re?" Tess asked Reneata one warm Thursday afternoon while they played checkers in the visitor's lounge. It was the only room at the hospital where the stench of bleach wasn't overwhelming, and the walls weren't covered in peeling beige and blue paint. It was Reneata's fifth day in the hospital. Ervin's funeral had taken place one day before, in the packed sanctuary of Gramps's church. His casket had been surrounded by his artwork, and the pews had been filled with mourning fans and supporters from across the state. Reneata decided not to attend. Instead, she took three sleeping pills, unbeknownst to her nurse, and slept the day away.

Tess sat anxiously, wearing a pair of denim shorts and a pink tank top that looked oddly like something from Reneata's closet. Reneata smiled when she saw her. Her baby sister was growing up so fast. A twinge of hopefulness filled her chest just knowing that she was doing okay after Ervin's death.

The oval-shaped space had three tables lined up down the center of the room. Around each table were four chairs, chained to the base of the table to help prevent the patients from throwing the chairs or falling out and hurting themselves. Each table had a game board made into the top surface. To play, patients had to sign a form at the main desk to get access to the game pieces. Oddly, every time Reneata had a visitor, the same red-haired nurse would stand behind the registration desk and ask her what year it was before handing her the game pieces. Then, she would follow up her silly question with a warning designed to stop Reneata from doing anything 'underhandedly un-appropriate' with the State of Alabama's property. Reneata would smirk, take the pieces, then return to her table while calling the red-haired nurse every nasty name she could muster in her head.

"What *isn't* that bad, Tess? Please don't let Gramps hear you say it that way."

"Being here," she nodded.

Shifting in her seat a bit to get comfortable, Reneata tried finding something in her sister's eyes to clue her into what she wanted to hear her say. But Tess was innocent – still a kid – and her intentions weren't hidden or easily misconstrued. "It isn't good, but it's just temporary," Reneata assured her.

"I forgive you," Tess said, almost in a whisper.

"For losing to you?" Reneata grinned as she watched Tess take her last black checker from the board.

"No, silly. For Ervin. For what happened with Byron. For anything you think was your fault."

Outside of her visits to the hospital's psychiatrist, no one had said anything to Reneata about what she told the mild-mannered cop on the day of the accident. It was slowly becoming another family secret that no one wanted to deal with. But Tess's innocence wouldn't let her play the harmful game of secret-keeping that so many black families played. She was naïve and ill-equipped to avoid mentioning the obvious. Instead, she did what an inquisitive and blameless soul would do – she led with the truth, which forced everyone around her to choose to walk in it, or to deny it.

Hearing her little sister mention Byron, made Reneata become flustered and angry. She was caught off-guard and unsure of what to say. Telling the cop – a stranger – about her past was one thing, but facing Tess was overwhelming.

Tess didn't know a life void of Ervin's addiction. Barely four, the night he first overdosed, her memories of him were filled with images of a willowy young man who stumbled through the old neighborhood like a zombie while she played in the park with her friends. Unlike Reneata, she never got to know and love his creativity, his wittiness, or the gentle way he cared for everyone around him. The drugs tore away all that was good about her big brother and left nothing but confusion. Although Tess's memories of Ervin weren't intact, she did have the misfortune of remembering the hard times the family endured when they were forced to leave the city after Reneata's fight with Byron. Tess would remember the months of living with Brad, Jo-Ann's old lover, and everything that happened during that rough period of their lives, creating another shameful reality that Reneata felt responsible for.

Eager to avoid the conversation, Reneata abruptly stood and motioned to the red-haired nurse that she wanted to leave the room. A surge of anxiety ran through her body. But when she stood, she realized that the young woman sitting across from her was her family, and not some stranger trying to hurt her. So, instead of leaving, she gathered the checkerboard pieces, then used the short walk across the room to gather her thoughts.

"You know I love you, right?" Reneata mustered the courage to say after returning to the table.

"Yea, of course I do," Tess said.

"I loved Ervin, too. What happened, you can't understand, and I can't explain it in a way to make you understand. But you got to trust me; I loved him, and I never wanted anything bad to happen to anyone."

"I believe you. Gramps, too. He's sad and struggling because we don't know who did this, and no one is sure if you or Byron had anything to do with it. But we want you home. Momma, too. I mean, she hasn't been here, I know. And she hasn't said much, but she loves you and she misses Ervin, a lot."

"Ervin was so sick... JoAnn tried to see about him. You couldn't understand, not now. Maybe, one day. I trust. One day."

Reneata was rambling, but the warm look in Tess's eyes told her that even in her confusion, she was happy to be there with her.

Reneata stood from the table, walked to Tess's side, kissed her on the check, and then told her something she should have told her long ago. "No matter what I did, and what people say about me, I'm not a bad person, and Ervin was never a bad person. Do you understand?"

Tess nodded in agreement, then hugged Reneata as if it were the last time they would see each other. Peering out of her hospital room window, Reneata watched as Tess drove off in Gramps's old pickup truck. She had just turned sixteen, and Reneata had missed her birthday.

More than a week had passed, and the police were no closer to solving the case than before.

"The Lucks brothers were in New York during the time of the murder," Officer Stewart told Reneata during his next visit.

"Check again. I just don't believe that," she said.

"We will continue to track down every lead while you focus on getting better. Have you spoken to your mother?"

Reneata shook her head, no.

"You should," he said. "She doesn't believe it's the Lucks Boys. She thinks it was someone else. We have a few leads, but they all have to do with Ervin's drug use and his time in prison."

"He was getting better. He hadn't used in months," Reneata insisted.

"I understand, but we have to follow up on everyone and everything and we will."

When Officer Stewart left the room, Reneata burst into tears. She wasn't convinced Byron wasn't to blame, and she refused to let herself believe it wasn't her fault.

CHAPTER 6: THE CALVARY

8 Days at Bethany Skylar

"What's in the 'old neighborhood' that you need to move away from?" Dr. Brown asked, in a thick New England accent that he tried hard to disguise. New to the hospital, a recent college-grad, Reneata had heard, and one damn good-looking shrink. After a week of mourning and glaring into the silence, for Reneata, he was a sweet distraction.

"What's in the 'old neighborhood? My life for the first twenty-four years. That's all," Reneata said sarcastically, while taking in the tiny size of Dr. Brown's office. His mahogany wood desk and oversized chair were too large to allow ample room for anything other than two small and uncomfortable hardback chairs for his patients, a short bookshelf, and an antique coat rack.

He can't be a day over twenty-five-years-old, she thought. Even with his big boy haircut and tortoiseshell-rimmed glasses. He looked like he'd sprung from the pages of a Ralph Lauren print ad and floated into that miserable place, thinking he would serve the world best by helping the poor and misunderstood. But looking at his intoxicating blue eyes, she knew his true gift was in the mirror, although she could tell he had no clue.

While she checked him out, he did the same. Peeking over the rim of his glasses, he watched as she took in the stuffiness of the office and read his educational accolades from Syracuse and Yale displayed on the wall behind him. Trying hard not to consider his eyes, she squirmed uncomfortably as he stared at the unorthodox way she wore her faded blue hospital-issued outfit.

Reneata sat unladylike in the hard-back chair. Her hair was in an untidy ponytail, and her face, that even on a lazy day would typically have a coat of makeup, was bare and stained with an inerasable frown. Her oversized t-shirt was tied into a knot across her stomach, exposing enough skin to capture the doctor's attention and showcase her belly ring. Rolled under at the waist, her straight-leg, drawstring pants were tightened nicely across her hips, exposing the small but firm roundness of her assets. Dr. Brown's eyes screamed *too much*. Maybe it was, but for the first time in a long time, Reneata didn't care about the world's unrealistic expectations of her.

They sized each other up like two prizefighters mere seconds after entering the ring.

Leaning forward on the wide mahogany desktop, and glaring directly into her eyes, Dr. Brown started talking. He had an hour a day, longer if needed, and another hour during group sessions every other day, to make Reneata tell him what made her life so insufferable that she had wanted to end it.

"But you said you lived elsewhere," he stated, in a nervous 'gotcha' tone.

"The old neighborhood *is* home." Her tone was so matter-of-fact that he pushed back from the desk and scribbled something on his little notepad.

"What were your ties to it?" he asked, just after returning to the halfway spot on the oversized desk, in yet a new tone of voice and demeanor – something akin to Perry Mason meets Jack McCoy. It was as if he were battling with himself right in front of her about who he was, the shrink, the interrogator, or just a silly guy with no clue about what he was doing.

"Everything. It's where I grew up. It's where I learned to be me."

"Give me an example?"

"Of what? Being me?"

"Yes. What's in the old neighborhood that makes Reneata

become the woman she is?"

Reneata was convinced the doctor was arrogant, and a bit self-righteous, and she needed to put him in his place. Gramps had taught her that ego and conceit were a thin veil over a weak man's insecurity. She didn't want his arrogance to make her feel more constrained in a place where she already had no freedom. In her own way, she was scrambling to take back small bits of her power. The power she'd start losing at 12 when Byron took interest in her, and throughout the years each time she made a poor decision. She no longer wanted her past, and now the suicide attempt, to define her. She didn't want to be pitied and looked down upon.

After leaning back in her chair and propping her dirty hospital-issued Converse on the edge of his desk, she decided to give him just what he expected.

"Do you like rap music?" she asked, now using the strength of her foot to rock back and forth in her chair.

"Somewhat?"

"Either you do, or you don't?"

"Not necessarily," he retorted, this time giving her an odd look.

"Not necessarily?"

"I can like some rap music but not all."

"Right. I forgot. Your profession teaches you to live in the abstract to keep the crazies from learning too much about you." Dragging her foot across his desk, she knocked a hand-painted coaster and a pack of black ink pens onto the floor.

"What does that mean, Reneata?" He responded with more uncertainty in his voice. He didn't appear fazed by her disregard for the things on his desk, but her questions were better than his, and that made him uncomfortable.

"Don't worry. I get it, you're too lame to understand rap music," she said jokingly.

"A bit unfair," he smirked, "but funny. Now, can we get back on track?"

For a second, she thought of standing and walking out of the room, just to ruffle his feathers, but decided against it.

"The origins of most rap lyrics are stories about the rapper's life. They are honest and gritty, vulgar and mean."

"And lies," he interrupted. "You do understand those stories often aren't true, right? Rappers make money by exploiting ghetto life…"

"And you know this because you lived in the hood?"

"No. But, I read…"

"Right. Not the point. I'm saying that the old neighborhood holds my story."

Shaking his head emphatically, he said, "Holds your story? I don't think you know what you're saying."

Don't know what I'm saying? she thought. *Is he serious?* "I'm sorry," she blurted in a high-pitched tone. "Was that too deep for you?"

"No. I just …" he stopped again before continuing. It was as if he'd made it to the final round of his favorite video game, but realized to win it all he needed to change his strategy. "Wait, Reneata. Let's start again."

"No need to," she said as she stood to leave. "You have a negative perception of me because I did this," she said angrily, raising her arm with the injured wrist, pointing it in his direction to show off her scars.

"That's not true," he insisted.

"Yes, it is. All you see is a poor black girl too stupid to

know anything. But what you don't know is that I learned to straighten my 'screets' long ago. My Gramps wouldn't have it any other way."

He pushed back in his chair, stared directly into her face, then tossed his ink pen to the desk. "I understand," he finally said, while inviting her to return to her chair with a slight wave of his hand. "Fair enough. I get it, and I'm sorry. What you are saying is that the girl with perfect grades who turned down three college scholarships isn't a dummy."

Reneata arrogantly clapped her hands to reward him as she took her seat.

He waited until she got comfortable before continuing his questions.

"Poor black girl? Is that how you see yourself?"

"Are you serious?"

"Of course."

"You telling me that the next question on your list of stupid questions is, do I believe I'm a rich white girl?"

"Wait. No," he said as he snickered quietly under his breath.

"I'm poor. I'm black. And I'm a girl. So yes, that's what I see."

"I don't see that," he stuttered. "What I'm trying to say is, I don't see a poor person; I see something else."

"What does poverty look like?" she asked sarcastically.

"Like need. I mean, like lack. I'm sorry, I'm not explaining myself well. Bottom line ... I don't see someone destitute."

"That's the problem. You see what I want you to see. And for the record, poverty has no physical description. I know you are smart enough to get that."

"Of course, because poverty is a state of mind."

"Are you asking me?" she blurted.

"No. I'm just saying that you are right; poverty has no physical description. But I'm not concerned with poverty. That's not why we are here."

"Doc, if you think poverty isn't the reason we are here, you need to go back to school."

He stopped, gave her an inquisitive look, jotted something on his notepad, then leaned back in his lounger like she'd given him something interesting to ponder.

The other shrink, Dr. Womack, was overweight, unattractive, and unusually hairy for a black man in his sixties. When he spoke, long veins of saliva connected the corners of his top and bottom lips. Reneata refused to say too much in his presence. He didn't seem to care, anyway. He would talk for thirty minutes without her saying a word, then excuse her to her room. It was different with Dr. Brown from the start – he was a conceited, young, white guy from an upper-middle class family in Massachusetts who could never understand her life. He made her feel uncomfortable and defensive on one hand. But on the other hand, and to her surprise, he made her wildly curious to get to know him better. Despite her bad manners, she liked Dr. Brown instantly.

Most mental health patients only received 72 hours of care at Bethany Skylar Institution. However, because of Dr. Brown, and Officer Stewart, who was a fan of Ervin's work, Reneata was given more time to heal and to get to the root of what happened to her on the day of Ervin's death. But unbeknownst to her – but not to Dr. Brown – there was a secret about the days leading to the tragic incident. Dr. Brown was on a mission to prepare Reneata for the pain she might face, when and if the secret was uncovered. From the start, he was convinced that his role in her recovery would be meaningful, but Dr. Brown, like so many others, had no idea how powerful secrets were when secret-bearers refused to grant them light.

CHAPTER 7: GOOD MAN

2002

An unusually hot day. Reneata greeted the sun wearing a canary yellow, strapless, sun dress and flip-flops. She always thought she was royalty in yellow, so she stretched her long neck and strutted through the parking lot of Piggy Mart grocery store, hoping to get the attention of a new guy she'd seen hanging around the old neighborhood.

Ty was working on the engine of a rusting 1988 Oldsmobile in the handicap parking space just outside the grocery store's entrance. His long cornrows framed his narrow, maple brown face, and almond-shaped hazel eyes. The hair at his temples wasn't nappy and wild, like it was on most guys with braids. It was slick, neatly lined, and calm. She could tell, even in his oil-stained, khaki, Dickie suit, he was gorgeous underneath.

What a beautiful lion, she thought as she passed by.

His boy, Drew, bumped Ty's side when she approached. Ty squinted to block the sunlight, then gave Reneata a quick, unimpressed glance. Avoiding feelings of sheer deflation, she flip-flopped past him with her head high, keeping her pride in check and continuing towards the grocery store doors. Turning to give him one last chance, she noticed an old man leaning on a red, chipped-paint bollard in front of the Oldsmobile. The beautiful lion was fixing this man's car. *Maybe the old man was his granddad or uncle*, she thought. But they didn't look anything alike. Where the beautiful lion reminded her of cocoa and vanilla cream, the old man, in his dusty house shoes with a hole in the toe, and a dingy, shapeless, white T-shirt, seemed sad and desperate.

The old man caught her attention - not because of his

handsome repair man - but because he was the perfect mascot for the old neighborhood. It was falling apart, one brick, one high-school dropout, one drug bust at a time. Tattered and torn, he, like so much she loved, had become irreparable.

After finishing her shopping, Reneata headed towards the checkout, toting a small black handbasket filled with groceries. Strolling mindlessly down the busy aisle, she clumsily walked smack into the backside of a heavy-set Nigerian lady next in-line at the checkout counter.

"Watch it," the lady groaned, with an accent as thick and course as an uncombed afro.

"Excuse me," Reneata said as the lady checked, then double checked her long Kenta cloth dress for evidence of soda and chocolate candy bar stains – the pre-purchased treats Reneata juggled in her free hand.

Rolling her eyes, the lady inspected the back of her dress with a swat of her hand. Thank God, she didn't find anything. There was something haunting in the creases of her thickly applied black lip-liner and bright-red lipstick.

Just as Reneata turned back towards her grocery basket, the lady caught her three-year-old daredevil son, who'd taken flight off the side of the basket and was falling into the candy rack.

"Get back in!" she yelled, barely lifting her teeth apart, barely moving her red-hot lips. Reneata had seen JoAnn do that trick many times before, and she knew it meant she was guaranteed a butt whipping before bed.

Smashing a loaf of bread and shuffling three cans of sardines with his feet, the little daredevil pushed out a loud grin as he pulled himself back into the basket.

JoAnn had given Reneata a list of five grocery items to pick up, and five dollars to spend. However, she had six items in her hand; a half-eaten candy bar in her mouth and an empty soda can at her feet. And to her luck, just as she reached down to push the can under the candy rack, avoiding the judging eyes of the young boy bagging groceries, someone pulled her hair, craning her neck and head toward the ceiling.

"What the hell!" she screamed while stumbling to get to her feet. She dropped the candy bar on the floor, kicked the soda can forward, barely missing the Nigerian woman's feet, and knocked over the handbasket.

Embarrassed and fighting mad, Reneata struggled to get her composure. When she did, she noticed the guy - the beautiful lion from under the Oldsmobile's hood - standing behind her.

"My bad," he said with a menacing look on his face.

Reneata was too busy scrambling across the floor while trying to keep her spilled, unpaid-for soda from attracting the store manager's attention. The lion stood watching her before reaching out his hand to help her to her feet.

"Are you crazy?" she angrily asked. "Don't touch my hair; I don't know you!"

"Like I said, my bad," he repeated, this time with a slither of sarcasm in his voice. His khaki Dickie's suit had a nametag stitched on the pocket that read Ty Jerome.

Reneata's once flirtatious eyes transformed into an angry stare. She realized how ridiculous she must have looked on the filthy floor of the grocery store. All because this guy – whom she now saw more clearly, had decided to pull her hair.

His dingy white T-shirt peeked from underneath his uniform, and he smelled of oil and rubber. Her fearless king of the jungle was nothing more than another brother with bad intentions.

"I saw you outside watching me," he said, so confident she wanted to slap him across the face.

"Are you kidding? I wasn't watching you; I was worried you were jacking the old man's car," she chastened.

"Jacking?" He snickered. "Little Miss Gangster in her yellow dress."

Rolling her eyes in his direction, she continued to clean up the mess he'd made. "You don't know me. Just don't touch my hair," she said.

"You in love with your hair, or something? It isn't all that. I've seen prettier."

"Prettier hair or prettier girls?"

"Both!" He moaned, and again, she rolled her eyes in his direction. Despite the frustration, Ty helped her pick up the tightly wrapped catfish nuggets and ketchup she was buying for that night's dinner.

"You go from Mr. Rude to Mr. Nice Guy. Why are you dogging me, than helping me clean up?"

Instead of answering, he finished picking up the items, placed the handbasket on the floor beside her, then stood to leave.

"This wasn't what I came in here to do," she heard him say, almost to himself.

Turning in her direction, he bowed like a court jester showing fake love to his ugly queen. "Forgive me for touching your precious hair."

Again, she rolled her eyes.

After picking up the handbasket, she returned to her place in-line, while Ty started walking towards the grocery store exit doors.

The cashier swiped, then bagged the groceries before telling Reneata the total amount.

"Seven dollars, twenty-six cents," the freckled-face, sandy-haired cashier said.

"For this?" Reneata shot back angrily, pointing to the items in the plastic bag.

"No, ma'am," he sang. And with a wave of his oddly long index finger, which, to her surprise, was painted with pink nail polish, he reminded her of just what she got. "You owe seven dollars and twenty-six cents for the nuggets," he pranced. "The ketchup. The lighter. The toilet tissue. The soda you drank coming down the aisle, and the candy bar you ate when you thought I wasn't looking."

Before Reneata could defend herself, she looked down and saw the candy wrapper under her shoe.

"Oh right," she said, now calm and a bit more respectful.

"But I only have five dollars."

"Then I guess you need to put something back," he insisted.

"I can't. My..." she stopped, realizing he didn't care about the details.

Just as she turned around to return the toilet tissue, Ty handed the cashier a ten-dollar bill and told him to give the change to "Little Miss Sunshine." Then he left the store.

As much as she didn't want to take it, Reneata knew JoAnn would give her hell all night if she came home without toilet tissue. Especially after Reneata refused to use the food stamps that JoAnn had left on the table for her. She hated shopping with food stamps. It was enough that the cashier always gave her a funny look when she pulled them out, but the way other people looked at her was worse.

Reneata took the change, tucked the groceries under her arm, and left the store.

When she passed Ty in the parking lot, she didn't look his way. The old man was still leaning on the bollard, and Ty's friend was talking to a girl on the opposite side of the car. Too embarrassed to say, 'Thank you,' she kept walking.

Three weeks later, they met again, but this time on the dance floor.

It was First Friday at Savoy's, and the ladies got in free. Reneata was feeling good after the two shots of Tequila she drank at home, and the two additional shots she had upon arriving at the club. Dancing in a circle of her girlfriends, and laughing loud enough for everyone to hear, she swirled right into Ty's arms.

"You again," he yelled over DJ Crush's reggae mix.

She laughed when she saw his face. He'd obviously been standing by, waiting to get her attention.

"You want to touch my hair again?" she said mischievously before giving him an awkward wink. Not sure why she did the latter, but the slight grin he gave her proved he got the joke.

"No. I mean," he stammered. "It's nice and all, especially tonight. I guess I was at a loss for words at the grocery store, and I did something stupid."

"That's cool," she grinned. "I never got to thank you for the soda and candy bar."

"You didn't, did you?" he smirked, before grabbing her hand and escorting her off the dance floor.

Ty walked Reneata to the bar and offered to buy her a drink. The bartender, a scrawny white girl with big green eyes traced in thick black eyeliner, caught Reneata's eye and nodded. It was her way of asking, without saying a word, if she wanted her usual shot of Tequila and lime juice.

"No thanks, I'm at my limit," she assured Ty while shaking her head to discourage the bartender from treating her like a regular. The bartender got the message, then turned towards Ty without looking Reneata's way again.

"That's nice," he said, as if assured that her response to the waitress was proof that the grocery store thief in the canary dress was a good girl after all.

Ty ordered a beer and a shot of whiskey before escorting Reneata to a U-shaped booth in the corner of the club, far enough from the dance floor that they could talk without screaming over the music.

Savoy's was a real hole-in-the-wall nightclub. Standing in front of the brick multi-unit commercial building, the only clue a person got that a gathering place existed was a single-door storefront entrance with the words Savoy's Café written in calligraphy on a small glass window. On both sides of the door were two storefront entrances. The one to the left read Bill's Hardware, a rectangle-shaped retail store, where you could order anything you needed to build, remodel, or dismantle a construction job. And the one on the right read Fabric Dime, a low-cost crafts and fabric distributor where half of the older women in the neighborhood spent their Saturday afternoons knitting and socializing. At night, when Bill's and Fabric Dime closed, Savoy's Café became Savoy's Place, known for its cheap specialty drinks and the best fried chicken platters this side of Mississippi.

The deejay - known as DJ Crush - stood behind an L-shaped table and two raised speakers. Around the dance floor were three high-top tables and one out-of-place booth on the opposite side of the room - the very spot Reneata was lucky enough that night to spend time with the handsome, but sometimes obnoxious, mechanic from the grocery store.

"Ask me how many times I thought of you since the day we met?" she said when they were comfortably seated.

"Why?" Ty asked, pretending to care more about the frothy foam on top of his beer than what she was saying.

"Because you insulted me, and I needed that."

"I didn't insult you," he said, before giving it any serious thought. "Well, it wasn't my intention anyway."

He placed his beer back on the table, then downed the shot of whiskey.

"Yea, you did, but that's cool," she replied.

Ty's corn-rolls were neat and quite mature for a 21-year-old man. His muscular body, designer jeans, and green fitted button-down caused the she-devil on her shoulder to squeal, "Damn!" Even the bartender was checking him out.

"Who could ever hurt the feelings of a lady brave enough to steal soda and a candy bar while wearing a bright yellow dress and flip-flops?" he said, and they both chuckled.

"I guess that wasn't a good first impression."

"No, it wasn't, but neither was touching your hair." There was something sweet and innocent in the abrupt happy in his smile when he apologized.

Gently touching his arm and leaning in towards him, Reneata said, "You know what they say about awkward beginnings."

"No. What do 'they' say?"

"It's sweeter to start again." Acknowledging the flirtatious look in her eyes, he placed the beer bottle on the table, wrapped his hand around her waist, and pulled her closer. "Let's do that," he agreed.

Reneata and Ty didn't stop talking until 4 o'clock in the morning. That was the beginning.

Over the next three years, they dated off and on. Ty was ambitious about the future. He wanted to take over his dad's car garage after serving a few years in the Army and getting a degree. Reneata cheered him on, but her goals were different. Keeping Ervin off the street and out of jail, and protecting Tess were the only dreams she'd ever had.

Ty cared about her like no other man had done, except Gramps. He made sure she ate right, exercised, and experienced new things. Every date was an adventure: they drove around the city listening to Coltrane and Miles Davis, made love in the park, and spent countless hours talking and planning their life together.

Despite Reneata's propensity for hanging out and drinking too much, he never left her side. He understood that she struggled with her past, her brother's addiction, and her mother. He was convinced his love and attention would give her the strength she needed to overcome these things. The many nights she stumbled out the doors of Savoy's Place, he was there, waiting to get her home and safely in bed. He was a 'good man'. And although, deep down in her heart, she desperately wanted someone to tend to her needs, she had no idea how to make a real relationship work.

Most of the women in the old neighborhood were single moms, working hard to raise their kids, or surrogate moms to a useless, ungrateful man. She'd witnessed good women sling some man's clothes from the porch, into the yard, set them on fire, then watch them burn before returning to her house like nothing had happened. She witnessed heartbroken mothers cry when the guy they loved, who seemed to love them and her kids, stopped coming around. When Reneata looked back, she realized she'd willfully entered a relationship equipped with nothing but attitude, misunderstanding, and guilt. She was nowhere near prepared to go to battle for love with the same strength or integrity it took to make it work.

Ty was different. His mother and father had been high school sweethearts who, somehow, made their marriage work for over thirty years. They beat the stereotypes of black love, battered back from his father's long bout with PTSD and alcoholism, and raised three kids who adored them. Ty was ready for a relationship, but she was not.

Ty adored Gramps. Treated Tess like she was one of his sisters and ignored JoAnn when she refused to get to know him at all. He knew about Reneata's past. He knew about Ervin's sickness; he often drove her to visit Ervin in jail, and promised to help him secure a job at the garage when he was released. But as kind and sweet as Ty was, Reneata took advantage of him.

One night - two years, five breakups and make-ups after they met, Reneata was at Savoy's Place with Sheila, a friend from high school. They were drinking and dancing with Darrin Levin and Theron Franks, two high school classmates they hadn't seen in years. Darrin, a tall, slim guy with light skin and gray eyes, invited Reneata back to his place for a nightcap. She and Ty had argued days before and were on a break. Ervin had been beaten half to death while in prison and was confined to the infirmary for weeks. JoAnn didn't want to talk about it. She wouldn't take any of his calls. So, Reneata did. Night after night, sitting in Jo-Ann's little kitchen, nursing a glass of vodka and listening to her brother cry.

The stress of everything had taken its toll on her. Her relationships were suffering, especially with Ty. Hanging out at Savoy's Place was her refuge. Carrying JoAnn's burdens and pretending to have the strength to save Ervin while still wanting to make a life for herself, was too much for her to handle.

So, that night, when Darrin invited her to his place, she accepted. But they never made it. Instead, they sat in his car in Savoy's parking lot, smoking weed and making out.

An hour passed. The passenger door to Darrin's car swung open, and Reneata fell out, landing on her knees on the cold asphalt. Laughing hysterically, and sloppy drunk, she scrambled to her feet. Struggling to get her blouse on and her skirt in place, she bumped into who she thought was a random person entering the club. But once she got her composure, she realized Ty was standing directly in front of her. His eyes, sad and disappointed, locked on Reneata.

After stumbling out the driver's side door with his jeans still undone, Darrin walked up to Ty. "What's up man?" he asked, so loaded he could barely talk.

Ty turned, then walked in Darrin's direction. Reneata expected him to punch Darrin in the face or drag her home in her drunken stupor, but instead, he stopped mid-way, looked back at her, then shook his head and quietly walked away. She leaned against the car, still trying to get dressed, expecting Ty to return and take her home. But he never returned. All those days, she had taken for granted that he understood why she did the things she did. That night changed everything.

Months passed, and Reneata didn't hear from him. He stopped coming around. He stopped caring whether she made it home from the club okay or if she was safe. She waited for the phone to ring. She looked for him in Savoy's, but he was nowhere to be found.

Going into the third month, she heard he had a new girlfriend. A 'nice' girl from a good neighborhood across town. Someone even told her he was happy. It killed everything in Reneata to know he'd moved on.

Ty was gone; he blew out of her life just as fast as he blew into it. How could she blame him? She was damaged goods. He deserved better.

More than six months passed, and she hadn't heard one word from Ty until the day Ervin got out of prison. The day Ty knew she needed him the most, he showed up at her doorstep, ready to make the hour drive. She hadn't heard his voice or smelled the light whiff of cedar wood that remained after he left the room in so long. But there he was, her beautiful lion, standing in the doorway, waiting to bring her brother home.

Ty didn't say a word about that night with Darren. He never asked for an apology. Instead, he told her he loved her, and that love was enough. After all those months, he came through for Reneata. No longer the beautiful lion with the braids, Ty had cut his hair into a neat close-cut fade and had lost a few pounds that he generously replaced with rows of muscle. He was so gorgeous, standing in her doorway, smiling at her, saying 'Hello," She knew from that moment on, they would be together. Somehow, they would make it work. They always found their way back to each other. He saw something in her worth holding onto.

When Ervin got out of prison, Ty was there, and the first-time he suffered a relapse, it was Ty who took him in and nursed him back to good health so JoAnn and Gramps wouldn't have to know about it.

To say Reneata was broken-hearted would be unfair. Broken-hearted was too minuscule of a word to define how empty she felt. She could never ask Ty to carry the burden of everything that happened during the nine days after he left for basic training. There was no way she could marry him now. He sought a better life for them, but she was still in the streets, breaking promises, and disappointing everyone in her path.

CHAPTER 8: THE PAST

Day 9 at Bethany Skylar
Journal Entry

Ervin created beautiful things. Like God masterfully creating the universe. He turned swirling atmospheres, stars, moons, suns, love, grace, chocolate, and rainbows into a colossal mass of wonder, then tossed them through the air and watched as they cascaded with no discernable direction, spilling out to fill every dark and quiet place with substance.

It was magnificent. He was magnificent. But he was never my creator.

JoAnn created me.

She took brown mud and spoiled milk and mixed it with a hint of cayenne pepper and cinnamon before splattering it against a brick wall. What she called art was nothing more than rigid and shapeless clay.

Confusion.

Inconceivable confusion.

"What does this mean?" Dr. Brown asked while thumbing through the journal he had given Reneata during their first session together. Most of the pages were filled with lists, heart-shaped scribbles, and incomplete pictures of sunsets.

"It's inspired," he added. "What made you write it?"

"Ty," she said in a sad tone.

"How so?"

"I miss him. I hurt him. I have brought nothing but confusion to his life and I don't know how to fix it."

"Why not start with talking with him?"

"No. That's not an option," she said.

"Why not?"

"Gramps often told me these amazing stories about traveling to distant places – Rome, Morocco, Africa, Iceland - and experiencing life unlike anything I could ever imagine. Each story ended in a beautiful love affair, but not the love of the opposite sex, the love of yourself."

"Your Gramps sounds like a great man," Dr. Brown said.

"You have no idea. He was trying to teach me something, give me something to hope for – to hold onto. I get it now."

"Of course he was, he loves you. But what does this have to do with Ty?"

"Ty knew my past and he still wanted to be with me. I was never as good to him as he was to me, but he loved me anyway."

"A love story," Dr. Brown said. "What about now?"

"Now. I'm here and he's out there hurting because of me."

"Reneata, why are you so convinced no one – JoAnn, Tess, Gramps, or Ty – can love you through this? You made a mistake. Have confidence you can get better."

Reneata sat back in her chair and stared at the ceiling as Dr. Brown's words ambled through her mind. All her life she'd never had so little confidence. She'd never felt so vulnerable. She was always the smart kid in the class and was rarely not the prettiest girl in the room. It was this confidence that attracted Byron and other guys like him. But her lack of life skills was what caused her to fall prey to bad decisions. Her mistakes had cost her so much. She knew, to heal, she needed to come clean. To face her own image in the mirror.

"Can I tell you something? It's personal," Dr. Brown asked.

"Of course," Reneata said.

"My younger sister, my only sister, Melissa, she was on drugs, too."

"What?" Reneata said, surprised.

"Yea. I try to never talk about. Although it led me to this profession. She was 18 when she started getting high, I was 20, in college, living my life. I had no idea things had gotten so bad for her. She was running away and ultimately, prostituting to buy drugs. My dad went bankrupt trying to get her help, but she never made it."

"What do you mean –she never made it? Did she die too? Did she OD?"

"She committed suicide, Reneata. She took her own life and she took my family's life with her."

"Oh my God. I'm so sorry … I didn't know…" Reneata dropped her head and began to cry. "I never expected you to understand, but maybe you do. Ervin was dying. I don't have to say it. You know. You witnessed it. It does something to you to see someone you love suffer so much."

"You want to believe they will be different." Dr. Brown's eyes kept a strong connection to hers.

"Beat down their demons," Reneata added, in a heartfelt way she later realized was their own personal language.

"Win," Dr. Brown finally said after a long pause. "You want to believe they will win."

Again, they shared that feeling; split it straight down the middle like a block of firewood. "Some do," Reneata added. "But the rest die. The question we are left with is how many will die with him? How torn apart can a family be before they can no longer mend?"

"Right, but families don't recover when someone they

loved dies." It was the final word on the matter for that day. Nothing left in the universe to say about death by addiction. Reneata and Dr. Brown were orphans of a painful experience. They shared that, along with so many other mothers, daddies, sisters, and brothers of addicts. Together they made up a family of unlucky thieves praying to steal one more day with the person they loved before the drugs took them away.

Dr. Brown's attention was having a positive effect on Reneata. She was finally ready to share her story and start the journey to getting better.

Five days after meeting him, two weeks after her suicide attempt, Reneata walked into his office and handed him a folded piece of paper. It was a list of things she wanted.

"This doesn't work that way," he said, staring up at her and attempting to return the list to her.

"I need it to. Can you help me?" she asked in a tone smothered with sadness, one that he hadn't heard before.

"Sit down. Give me something I can use to help you. Tell me your story and I will do everything I can to get you out of here, happy and healthy."

She shook her head in agreement. Took a seat and began to tell Dr. Brown her story.

CHAPTER 9: LUCY

Day 16 at Bethany Skylar

"I killed my brother," Reneata said as Dr. Brown slowly pulled his note pad from the drawer. "It started the day after Cortez, a boy in the old neighborhood, kissed me under the big oak in our yard." Pausing for a bit - long enough to remind herself that once she started down this trail of confessions, there was no way back.

"And," Dr. Brown blurted, anxious to get things moving. He knew his time was winding down with her. The hospital would only let her stay for 21 days, and she was five days away from returning home.

"And, the day after, I lost my virginity to Byron. He was twenty-one at the time."

Dr. Brown's eyes widened, then narrowed. He sat back in his chair, then uncomfortably leaned his body forward, like the starter gun had sounded but there was cement in his running shoes. "You told me about the kiss, you told me a little bit about Byron, but you never mentioned he was twenty-one-years-old."

The doctor's expression made Reneata cringe. She felt dirty and guilty. It was the sting of judgment that she hated most. It was a reminder of how different they were – his maleness and her femaleness. His whiteness and her blackness. His wealth and her meekness. They were not two sides of the same coin, as she may have thought. In many ways, their lives were contradictions of one another.

"Maybe 'loss' is the wrong word," she finally blurted. "At the age of 12, the only things a little girl should worry about losing are hair barrettes and earrings." The barrenness of her words brought an uneasy calmness in the room. They both welcomed it. For the first time, she wasn't trying to hide behind sarcasm and phony confidence, she was being real. She was letting him see her vulnerability.

Dr. Brown stood, walked around his desk, then sat in the chair next to Reneata.

"Can I hold your hand?" he asked. Without thinking, she said yes. She wasn't quite sure why, but it was the perfect thing to do. Plus, she desperately needed to be touched. Her body longed to feel the warmth of another person.

His demeanor changed. He stopped being at war with himself. Dr. Brown struggling with Mr. Brown to determine who was most needed at that moment. When his eyes softened, she knew the right one had shown up. He was ready to listen, and she was finally ready to let him in.

Reneata's friend, Lucy, lived a half-mile from the old neighborhood in an out-of-place, three-story duplex that stood between a run-down church and an abandoned lot where an old brick house once stood. Inside the duplex, it was cold and dusty. The front room was sparingly decorated with old furniture, and the walls were blank, while the bedrooms had mattresses on the floors and space heaters for warmth. The loneliness of the house made it hard to believe Lucy lived there with her mother, three brothers, and two cousins.

Ms. Cynthia, Lucy's mom, looked much older than thirty-eight. JoAnn would always say that Cynthia got lost somewhere around thirty-five years-old, when she began to lose a battle with her three boys – Byron, Randall and Leon - because each one was spending less time in school and more time on the streets, peddling drugs and gang-banging. The result of their mischief was a small and timid mother who was looking for a second chance to get it right with her nine-year-old daughter, Lucy.

JoAnn had known Ms. Cynthia since elementary school. She, Tess, and Reneata often stopped by Cynthia's house after church for a slice of cake, and they invited Lucy to their house for sleepovers. Ms. Cynthia was a bit strange and was never a big talker. She had her first son at fourteen, her second at sixteen, and the third at nineteen. No husband, no formal education other than learning to bake, learned from her grandmother. When she wasn't working the morning shift at the Dollar Store, she sold freshly baked cookies and cakes from her house to pay bills.

Her life was tough. Like JoAnn, and so many of the women in the old neighborhood, she was hardened and cold but unrelentingly strong. JoAnn called it *black woman strong*. They'd survived slavery, discrimination, intimidation, and poverty. They were pushed down, put down, and degraded, and yet they still wore their crowns, took care of their families and fought for what was right. Although Reneata agreed with this depiction of black womanhood, she wasn't convinced JoAnn lived up to her own standards, and watching Ms. Cynthia's frail body walk the halls of her empty house made Reneata wonder if a black woman's strength was more of a curse than a blessing.

Reneata had heard about Lucy's brothers on the street but she'd never met them until the day of Lucy's birthday party.

JoAnn dropped off Reneata and Tess at Lucy's house early so she could go spend time with her new beau. Upon entering the house, Ms. Cynthia invited Reneata to join her in her bedroom. Reluctantly, Reneata followed her, while Tess, who hated birthday parties, took her Dr. Seuss book into one of the vacant bedrooms upstairs.

Lucy and the other guests were in the basement, playing. Every few seconds a wave of screams came from the bottom of the house as Lucy – the self-appointed boogie man - entertained everyone.

Ms. Cynthia's bedroom was no different from the rest of the house, apart from a mirror propped against the wall, and a picture of Lucy on a small table in the corner. The only thing out of place was Reneata, standing with her arms wrapped around her little waist. Curious about what Ms. Cynthia needed from her so desperately. What was so pressing that Ms. Cynthia couldn't wait until later, when JoAnn returned?

Seconds after entering the room, Ms. Cynthia clapped a key into Reneata's hand and looked her dead in the eyes. "I'm leaving, lock the door behind me, and don't open it for anyone, not even my boys."

A bit confused, Reneata listened intently, then followed Ms. Cynthia back into the front room. Strapping a black bag over an old, torn, leather jacket, Ms. Cynthia headed for the door, clearly on a mission.

Reneata locked the door behind her, then watched from the bay window as the woman's frail body disappeared into the shadow of the vacant lot next door. Two men leaning against a broken fence in the rubble followed her into the darkness seconds after she passed by.

An hour later, Reneata was still glued to the window, waiting for Ms. Cynthia to emerge from the lot with a bag filled with ice cream and cookies - her alibi for leaving a twelve-year-old in charge of a house filled with screaming kids. But there was no sign of her, and Reneata was nervous and ready to go home.

The smell of weed was intoxicating as it poured in from the back porch, where Lucy's brothers had gathered. Their laughter could be heard through the sporadic screams of the birthday boogieman in the basement as she terrorized her guests. Hearing them, pushed Reneata's heart rate higher and triggered a panic that only a young girl abandoned in a house full of boys she did not know could feel.

Scouring the vacant lot for one glimmer of Ms. Cynthia, or the men she had left with, Reneata didn't hear Byron when he walked into the room.

"What's your name?" The unfamiliar voice startled her as

she turned from the window to see Lucy's middle brother standing in the doorway of the kitchen. Barely two feet taller than Reneata, he stood erect, chest pronounced, at attention.

She turned his way, then hesitated before squeaking her name in the most unsettling voice she'd ever heard come from her little mouth. "Can I call you Re?" he asked with a smile in his voice that she could only imagine was brought on by how uncomfortable he made her.

Barely raising her eyes, she said nothing. Instead, she returned to the bay window, praying to see Ms. Cynthia, so she could call JoAnn to come to pick them up.

Byron kept talking, but she didn't turn around. She knew it was rude, but he was twenty-one, and the most handsome guy she'd ever seen. What could he say to her with that big voice that sounded nothing like most boys she knew? It was an unusual, New York via dirty South, accent that she loved instantly.

"Not Re, but Reneata," she squeaked, to reassure him and almost remind herself. For some reason, everything simple became hard to do. Like the first time her math teacher called her to the blackboard to explain how many times three divided into 364. As simple as the problem was, being at the blackboard in front of everyone created an unexplainable fear. Today was no different. Byron caused her to question who she really was.

With Reneata still refusing to turn in his direction, Byron walked up behind her and touched her hair. For the first time, there were no ponytails and hair barrettes. JoAnn had let her wear it down, and to everyone's surprise, it brushed the center of her back in big curls that took three hours to perfect. She'd chosen her own outfit for the first time, pairing a fitted denim skirt with the pink sweater Gramps gave her on her last birthday.

"You twelve?" he asked, and she shook her head, yes, again, this time raising her eyes only a few inches higher than before, and turning in his direction.

"You don't look twelve," he blurted as if it were a rite of passage.

"I am," she assured him. Convinced it would prompt him to run back to his brothers, who now sounded more like a pack of mean girls taunting the defenseless than a troupe of public enemies.

"I'm Byron." He took her hand and held it while he checked her out. "Why you here with these kids?"

"Ms. Cynthia invited my sister and me."

"Them kids, you much older."

"Just a couple years."

"Look at you." He gave her a second once-over. "You need to be out back with the grown folks."

Unconvincingly, she said *no,* and he smiled.

"Nobody gone bother you, girl. You trust me, right?" He was sweet mugging her into submission, and she didn't know how to say no.

"Mr. Byron, I can't. Ms. Cynthia made me promise to watch the door." Her voice shook as rapidly as her knobby knees.

"'Mr. Byron', I like that," he said. "How old you think I am?"

"At least twenty."

"Yea, I'm twenty-one and you twelve. That's only a few years."

"You older than my brother. I mean I can't be hanging with you. Plus, I got to watch the door. Ms. Cynthia said…" but before she could finish, he grabbed her hand and pulled her towards the kitchen. She stumbled along, petrified.

Before she knew it, she was sitting in his lap in a circle of boys. The smell of weed hovered in the air. Whether she chose to or not, they each took turns slowly inhaling relics of every puff of weed. Byron and his brothers washed down their turn with a shot of liquor.

When Byron spoke, his words swung in the air like acrobats traversing the high wire under the big tent at a circus. Everything he felt, he said. Some of it made little sense to Reneata until it caught the arms of its high-flying partner. He was the first boy she had heard spit verses of rap lyrics while talking about the beauty of his high.

"I remember the mutherfuckin' sky lit-up like the Fourth. No, New Years. Fuck New Years, the Fourth. With those sparkles and shit. Had me peddling cross the Lantic without a boat. I was high, high, so high I could touch the sky. You feel me?"

His brothers wouldn't blink until he finished. It was like he was speaking some foreign language that everybody wanted to learn.

He would talk with no pause. It was mesmerizing. Especially to Reneata. He was different. Street smart and unapologetic. Unlike the other boys who tried to act and dress like a New York rapper, Byron had this KRS-One from the Boogie Down vibe. He sported a black and white leather bomber jacket, Malcolm X t-shirt, and a leather Kangol; it was his signature style. As she got to know him better, she realized that his brothers, even the eldest, envied him.

He talked on and on about 'juvi' and 'dime bags,' 'swithin' and 'trap hoes'- things she knew nothing about. But he had this way of making everything sound like Disney World.

"Wait," Dr. Brown interrupted. "Why did any of this mean something to you? You were twelve years-old."

Subdued and anxious to tell the story, Reneata stared into

the distance before responding. "Byron was painting a beauti-fully-flawed picture on a white canvas."

"And you were the young and innocent canvas?" Dr. Brown asked.

"Yes. I realized when I got older that although I was afraid of him, I thought being around a guy like Byron would set me apart from the other girls. He created a picture of a world that was exciting and unfamiliar to me. He was different from any guy I'd ever met. I knew things at twelve that I shouldn't have known, and I felt things about myself and the world I was grow-ing up in that I shouldn't have had to feel at that age."

"What did that mean to you?" Dr. Brown asked.

"Somehow the idea had been planted in my head that who was on my side said as much about who I was, as who I was in the inside," she said. "Byron intrigued me from the moment we met. He was like a new toy or my favorite song on the radio. I don't expect you to understand but I wanted to be connected to some-thing, someone. It's human nature to want to be loved. I was no different than anyone else. I wanted to feel like someone's most precious possession. I didn't get that from my mom, and I never knew my dad. Byron gave me something that I really thought was special. But believe me, I know better now. When I have girls of my own, I will teach them to paint their own picture. I will protect them and teach them to love themselves. I will give them better opportunities."

Dr. Brown shook his head in agreement, then encouraged her to keep going.

CHAPTER 10: INNOCENCE

All while Byron spoke, Reneata swatted his hands under the table as they slowly moved up her thigh. Her little body swarmed in his lap, just enough to keep from feeling anything other than the boniness of his leg. But she was too afraid to get up. She didn't know what he or his brothers would do to her.

"Look at this B here. Somethin' else, ain't she? Like a little spray of sunshine sitting on my lap." His brothers laughed.

"What's your name again, Sweetie?" Randall asked.

"Reneata."

"We gon call you Re when you ready and Sweet-Thang when you not," Byron said, and his brothers chuckled impishly at her expense.

When Byron's high settled in and the grip on her leg loosened, Reneata got the courage to wiggle from under the table and spring from his lap. Before he could catch her, she quickly sprinted into the house to find Tess so they could walk home.

Tess was playing Ms. Pac Man in one of the upstairs bedrooms. "You ready to go?" Reneata asked, anxiously, but Tess didn't hear her, nor did she look up. Before Reneata could call her name again, Byron snuck up behind her, planted his wide hand over her mouth, then dragged her from the room.

Before she knew it, Reneata was in a room somewhere on the bottom floor of the house.

It was less of a bedroom and more like an oversized closet with a twin-size mattress on the floor and a small window just above ground level. Cool air raced in but not enough to thin the smell of sweaty socks and stale beer. Dingy white sheets were crumpled on the mattress, and an unzipped red backpack filled with what looked like little plastic bags stuffed with folded aluminum foil lay behind the door.

By the time she wrestled his hand from around her mouth, her skirt was undone, and Byron's arm was tangled in her pink sweater.

"That's all you got?" he mocked.

"Get off me! Please get off me!" The random screams of Lucy and her guests made Reneata's cries difficult to be heard.

"Let me go, Byron! Please, let me go!" she pleaded again. She didn't understand what was happening. She couldn't judge his intentions.

To her surprise, the more she cried, the looser his grip became, but she was still under his control.

"Can I call you, Re?" he repeated over and over.

"That's not my name!" Reneata screamed, and fear shuddered her little body like a subway barreling through a tunnel.

"You mad, Re-nea-ta. Ms. Re-nea-ta..." he gave her every syllable slowly, followed by a wide-mouthed grin that he hid by turning his head and pretending to cover his mouth with his shoulder. Between struggling to get free and listening as he poked fun at her name, the tears began to flow. This wasn't like the kiss from Cortez the day before. This was something else, something she was too naive to understand.

When she stopped fighting him, he let her go. Still unsure of his intentions, she took her clothes and balled up into a fetal position in the corner of the room.

When he made no move in her direction, she started to dress in haste. Falling back on the mattress, he watched her in complete awe. The lily-white training bra JoAnn had brought her weeks before was slightly torn. Her clothes were wrinkled, and there were no curls left in her hair. She fought back a rush of tears long enough to get her clothes on.

When everything was intact, and she was moving toward the door, ready to flee from that house with every ounce of energy she could muster, Byron did something she wasn't expecting. He crawled on his knees, grabbed her by her waist, pulled her to him, then tucked his head into her stomach. "You so young and pretty. Smell so good." He spoke as if she were a figment of his imagination, like he was thanking the universe for granting him something he'd dreamed of a million times.

His body clung to hers until he felt her heartrate simmer to a normal pace. He became innocent and weak in that moment, nothing like the brute who dragged her to the basement. Somewhere between distress and curiosity, Reneata stopped being afraid. Maybe it was the stories she'd heard other girls her age tell about their first time with a boy. There was nothing sweet and tender about losing your virginity. It was an experience many girls longed to forget yet were willing to repeat if it meant they could keep some boy's attention.

Byron kissed her several times on her neck – it felt nothing like JoAnn had warned her of, and yet, another first. It was as if a switch had gone off in his head, and he'd realized there was more power in his gentleness than in making her afraid.

Dr. Brown's hand felt unusually warm at that moment. Reneata couldn't pull loose; he must have expected her to try, so he repositioned his hand to hold on tightly by placing his fingers just above the scar on her wrist. It was a message, and Reneata heard it loud and clear. The real scars she carried had little to do with her wrist; the real scars were all the memories she hadn't shared with anyone.

His expression alone urged her to go on.

"Before I knew it, Byron was inside of me. I remember thinking, do I want this? How do I stop it? Should I stop it? But the kisses kept coming, one at a time. For as much as I didn't know what I was doing, at that moment, I felt it was the best thing I'd ever done."

"Wait," Dr. Brown interrupted her. He wanted her to explain, but she refused to stop talking. She knew he didn't understand, and that was ok.

Byron's body, moving slowly and intentionally, to test how Reneata would react, rose, then fell, over and over. When she didn't run, when she didn't scream, he kept going. When she didn't fight, he kept going until there was a knock at the window.

"Shhh!" he said, quickly rolling to the side. He kneeled near her, placed his hand over her mouth, then pushed her against the wall.

While buckling his pants with one hand, he raised the window with the other.

"What's up?" he said, speaking in a tone that assured her he wasn't surprised to see his visitor.

"You know what's up, B?" Reneata heard a male voice say. The window was grungy and small, making it difficult for her to see the person's face but she could see his shoes and the bottom of his jacket.

"How much?" Byron asked, still buckling his pants.

"Three rips, four tags," the guy said.

"No bartering this time, B. This ain't the fucking wild west."

"I got cash."

"Good."

Byron slammed the window shut, took three red and four

blue bags from the backpack on the floor. He looked her way, only briefly reminding her with his eyes and the nod of his head to remain quiet.

In a voice that seemed oddly familiar, the guy called to Byron through the shut glass, twice, before his package was ready.

"What the hell wrong with you, man? Stop calling my name. This ain't your first time. Don't make me come out this room and jack you up!" Byron's voice echoed through the house while the man fervently paced, like a kid waiting to tear open his illicit Christmas gift.

Byron slid open the window and pushed the screen out just wide enough to take his money.

"Twenty, thirty, forty..." He stopped short of fifty. "Who you fooling? This ain't enough."

Shifting from one foot to the next, the guy insisted, "I'm good for it, B. You know me..." This time his voice was so familiar Reneata raised her body forward to take a look. There was nothing special about a pair of boots that every guy in the neighborhood had, but that jacket and the hollowness of his voice...

Before she could get to her feet, Byron pushed her square in the middle of her chest and pointed his finger inches from her face. "Get down!"

She froze.

"Who that, B?" the guy in the window asked nervously.

"Nobody."

"No, for real, who that? I can't be here. Whoever that is, you better have 'em in check."

"I got this," Byron said, then took one of the blue bags and two of the red bags and tossed them back into his stash. The five remaining were slid under the screen, and the window slammed shut.

"Bounce, homeboy!" He waved his hands as if they were capable of magically causing his customer to disappear.

When Reneata knew the coast was clear, she crawled out of the corner and started to get dressed. "Not you, sweetheart," he turned in her direction, now pulling at his buckled pants. But JoAnn's words were slowly wrapping themselves around her cold body -- *Neta, if you don't know what you got, you gon give it away.* Something else she finally understood.

"I need to go...and find my sister," she stuttered.

"We were making progress. You liked it, I could tell." His mood shifted like a race car barreling down a crowded two-lane track – one moment he was angry, the next, he was not.

"What's your favorite story?"

"What you mean?" Reneata asked nervously.

"What's your favorite story, sweetheart?" he asked again.

"You mean like Cinderella?"

"Yea, like Cinderella. She's tight, just like you, hot B, a real cutie, looking for her knight in shining armor. You believe in that, right?"

She nodded her head, feeling a bit undone by the way he stroked her hand and looked her directly in the eyes.

"She got the glass slipper. You remember that?"

She shook her head, yes, again.

"Your momma told you it's fantasy? Not to believe that you can get a glass slipper -- *little black girls from the hood can't be princesses?* She told you the Lucks boys are bunk, and she gon beat you down if she ever caught you with one of us?"

Reneata stared without responding.

"Your momma don't know nothin' about the Lucks boys.

We take care of our own. We love our women. Family first. You stick with me, and you will get your glass slipper. You understand?"

Again, the dumb girl showed up. His mouth moved, and Reneata was enthralled. The words didn't matter. She was now *his* girl. She had never been anyone's girl before.

"My momma and Tess are looking for me," she finally said.

"Nobody else is coming to the window so don't worry."

"It's not that. I'm ready to go." She started towards the door until she came upon Byron's red book bag on the floor. She wouldn't dare step over it. She didn't know what he would do. But she thought of the guy at the window, how familiar his voice had been.

Before she opened the door, she turned toward Byron. "Who was that at the window? He sounded like somebody I know. He sounded like…"

"Your *brother*. That was E, my best customer. I guess I'm not the only one with a fucked-up family!" Byron released a gush of laughter that sent chills up her spine.

"No!" she cried. "No! That was not my brother. He wouldn't…"

"He would, he does, he is, fill in the blanks little girl, it's all true. Ervin the Great, Alabama's own JJ Evans is a crack head."

"My brother is not a crack head! That's not true! Take it back!" Reneata rushed towards him. He rose from the mattress and caught her by the arm. It was at that moment that she lost it. She was kicking and scratching like a wild person. And all he did was laugh.

She didn't even know what a crack head was. All she knew was they took drugs - they lived for them.

All the hours she'd spent running through Ms. Cynthia's

house as a little girl on Sunday afternoons. She, Lucy, and Tess playing tag in the basement. Lucy's brothers were never around. Between long stays in county jail or hanging in the streets, she'd never seen anything more than pictures of them when they were innocent little boys. And there she was losing her virginity to one of them, the same one that sold drugs to her brother.

"When I stepped out the door, Byron slammed it shut behind me so hard the wind seemed to usher me forward."

"Enough," Dr. Brown said without releasing her hand. "You and the dope boy had sex?"

"Yes. That's when it started."

"A relationship, or Ervin's end?"

"Both."

"Look at me," he demanded when he saw her head tilt towards the floor. "What happened next?"

"The next year, just around my thirteenth birthday, I found out I was pregnant. Byron didn't want the baby. I ended up having an abortion in some rat-infested back alley clinic."

"Did JoAnn know?"

"She knew something was up with me, but she was too busy trying to keep up with Ervin to pay attention. My stomach was growing. I was thirteen. Scared. All my nightmares came true. I ended up on the wrong end of a dirty knife. I've hated myself for that ever since."

"What about Byron? Did you hate him? Did he earn your hate? What about the drugs? Ervin?"

"At thirteen, Byron earned my undeniable adoration. I was a fool, a dumb girl. He sold that junk to my brother for years. I helped him. That's what I'm most guilty of."

Dr. Brown fell back in his chair. "You supplied drugs to your own brother?" The expression on his face was the judgment she feared most. They sat in awkward silence for a while. She knew she needed to explain. Maybe she just needed to hear her explanation out loud and to try to see if there was a chance that she could one day forgive herself.

CHAPTER 11: LOYALTY

"Three knocks. Never a fourth. Three knocks on the wall that separated our bedrooms, then complete silence. Typically, on a Friday night. JoAnn would be out partying, Tess would be at Gramps's house, and me and Ervin were home alone, secluded behind closed bedroom doors. Three knocks and I'd know it was bad," Reneata explained.

"Whatever I was doing, I would stop, find my favorite Teddy bear, Ernie, and pull apart his cottony belly through a small slit I'd cut in his side. Tucked in the softest part of the bear was a wad of wax paper with a few pills in it."

"What kind of pills?" Dr. Brown asked.

"Byron called them, *heroin tablets*. He convinced me they were pain pills used to help addicts recover. But I learned when I was older, they were Diamorphine. A lethal dose. Byron wanted to keep Ervin happy so that I would be in debt to him. I was young, I didn't understand back then, but now, when I look back, I realize how evil Byron was and how stupid I was for helping him."

"Ervin learned about me and Byron's relationship shortly after it started. He never said a word to me about it. Instead, we shared those three knocks. They were retribution for a million poor decisions."

"Did it help?" Dr. Brown asked.

"Yes. For a while at least. See, after I gave Ervin the pills, the next day he would go to Gramps's place and create something. Like his old self. He would bring it home, and JoAnn would be so excited. So hopeful. She would forget that the day before, he was stealing money from her purse. And the day before that, he had gone missing or was found overdosed in a friend's house. Or the day before that, he'd lied about something ridiculous or destroyed something important. I thought I was doing good. I didn't know any better."

"How did you get the drugs?"

"I would do favors for Byron."

"What type of favors?"

"You know. Favors," Reneata said, clinging to her last morsel of dignity.

"Sex?"

She shook her head, yes.

"Did you sell for him?"

She shook her head, yes, again.

"What else?"

"I stole things. I hooked up with his friends – whatever it took to make him happy and make Ervin healthy again."

"You were loyal?" Dr. Brown said, trying to rationalize what she'd done.

"Well, yes. I had no choice."

"Wait. You did have a choice. Why would you say that? Why be loyal to a man who rapes you, gets you pregnant, then forces you to have an abortion? Who puts a young girl on the streets and forces her to have sex and run drugs. Why be loyal to a brother who needed a fix so bad he would take drugs from his little sister?"

"Rape?" she questioned, snatching her hand from his grasp. "Byron never raped me. I let him. And I wasn't a prostitute. You're getting this all wrong."

"You were twelve."

"So! I knew what I was doing."

"Listen to yourself. The day before this jerk raped you, you kissed a boy for the first time under a tree in your mother's yard. You didn't even know how to handle the kiss, let alone navigate sex with a twenty-one-year-old."

"But I didn't say no. I didn't stop him."

"You were scared, Reneata. Just like you are now, covering up for someone else's wrong doing."

"I'm not covering up for Byron. I told the police everything I knew. I want him caught."

"No. You want to get caught. You want to be forgiven. The guilt is destroying you from the inside out. There's no proof this is about Byron or his brothers. Your brother lived a hard life that hurt a lot of people, including you. You were a misguided kid who found solace in the arms of a man who gave you the attention you needed."

"Stop, please. I'm done!" They were already into their third hour, and she was exhausted. The nurses had changed shifts while they talked.

"Okay. Fine. I will stop. Until tomorrow," he said, rising from the chair next to Reneata and returning to his desk, unfazed by the sweat and exhaustion on her face. "This was good."

"For you, maybe."

"No, for you," he assured her.

CHAPTER 12: DADDY

Day 17 at Bethany Skylar

The walk from Dr. Brown's office back to the patients' quarters was cold and lonely. It was three floors and fifty-seven steps from his office door to the dingy confines of Reneata's stale-smelling room.

Rape. That was crazy, Reneata thought. Every girl she knew had sex too soon with a boy who never gave her no-never-mind twenty-four hours later. It wasn't rape; it was a bad decision. At least Byron stayed around. It wasn't a one-time thing.

"You are leaving me with nothing," Reneata said as she entered Dr. Brown's office for their next session.

"What are you talking about?" he asked, barely looking up from a stack of papers attached to a clipboard.

"My childhood was not what I remember it to be."

"I'm good, Reneata, but I can't change the past or the future," he said, still looking at the papers.

"Yes, you can," Reneata insisted.

Dr. Brown put down his papers and looked her in the eyes. "How, tell me?"

"You make people see things differently. You make us face the sadness."

"I want you to face the truth, Reneata. This is not to hurt you," he assured her. "What did you remember that made you sad?"

"Not so much sad, but you got me thinking."

"About what?"

Dr. Brown stood behind his desk to do what appeared to be stretching his leg. His eyes never left hers.

Following his mannerisms, Reneata straightened her back, then relaxed her shoulders. They were subconsciously preparing for another long day of discovery – there was so much more to cover.

"You never told me why you and JoAnn don't get along," Dr. Brown said.

"No, I haven't."

"Would you like to talk about it?"

"Honestly, no. But I'm sure that won't satisfy you."

Slightly grinning, Dr. Brown nodded his head in agreement. "Let's start there."

Reneata paused for quite a while before saying a word. She'd never told a soul about her feelings towards her mother. Not even Ty.

"My mother slept with Byron," Reneata finally said.

"What? How did that happen? Why?" Dr. Brown asked insistently.

A single tear ran down Reneata's face.

"The night Byron attacked me. The night I defended myself by cutting him with the key. It was that very night when I discovered a piece of my mother's jewelry on the floor next to Byron's bed. That's what we were fighting about."

"Byron said a million times how he wanted to sleep with my "fine ass, momma," but I never thought it would happen. She pretended to hate him. I didn't think she knew about us. We were so low-key, never talking during the day, only hooking up at night. I ran drugs for Byron, but I wasn't hanging on the street corners as you may think. I really thought we were being discreet."

"When you confronted her, what did she say? Did she admit to it?"

"She said, 'your so-called boyfriend got your brother strung out on drugs. You watched it happen – you helped him. What kind of sister are you?'"

Shaking her head profusely, Reneata struggled to explain away JoAnn's accusation. "She was right. I had no real explanation for what I'd done. But she had no explanation for what she'd done, either. I remember screaming at her, 'you slept with my boyfriend - half your age, what kind of momma are you!'"

"She smashed her cigarette into an empty beer can, stood, and walked within a foot of me. I remember her saying, 'the kind of mother that cares enough to do anything to keep that animal from between her daughter's legs and pumping dope in her boy's arm."

"She did it to help you? To stop him from hurting you?" Dr. Brown asked.

"Yes. That's what she said, but it didn't make any sense. She went on and on about Byron promising her that if she slept with him, he would leave me alone and stop selling to Ervin. It was ridiculous!"

"Ok, Reneata. Stay calm, what happened next?"

"She found out about the fight I had with Byron that night and how his brothers threatened me. She was so angry and afraid that she made me and Tess pack a bag, and we traveled a few hours south of Tinsley to one of her friend's place, Mr. Brad. We stayed with him for months without returning home. She knew that Byron and his brothers had a reputation for hurting people especially when you crossed them. She wanted to protect us."

"This incident strained your relationship with your mother and put your family in danger. What about Gramps and Ervin?"

"Gramps didn't come. He supported my mother. He never knew about her relationship with Byron, but he knew about me and Byron, and he wanted us to be safe. Ervin stayed too. It didn't take long before he was in trouble, doing time for a robbery in the neighborhood."

"So, your mother uprooted you and your sister and took you to live with a stranger. How did that work out?"

"Let's just say, Mr. Brad was a good guy for a while, until his sexual needs were no longer being met by JoAnn. He kicked us out after about six months. After a few days of living in the car, we returned to Tinsley. Byron and his brothers were nowhere to be found but I knew we would never be safe."

CHAPTER 13: MORE DEBT TO PAY

Day 19 at Bethany Skylar

It's funny how sadness never gets a front seat.

How despair must lurk around like a ghost instead of standing firmly in the middle of our living rooms.

Why is it that a broken heart isn't worn around our necks on a shiny gold chain?

If we could expose our pain sooner maybe it wouldn't rob us of time. Especially when you would, if the choice was yours, spend every hour swinging towards the heavens at the park or laughing until the creases of your jaws ached.

When I look back on those years, I miss my family, back when JoAnn was 'momma' and we had so little guilt. I miss all those things my life had no time for.

"Thank you for sharing. This is helping you explore what is void in your life." Dr. Brown closed Reneata's journal and handed it back to her. "I hope you keep writing when you return home."

Reneata nodded her head in agreement.

"Can I ask you something, and I need you to be honest?" Dr. Brown insisted.

"Yes," she said.

"How did all of this make you feel?"

Reneata sat back in her chair for a while before answering. Her body had shrunk to just under one-hundred pounds. The medical doctors were concerned, and so was Gramps. She hadn't looked at her image in the mirror in days because she couldn't bear to. She couldn't eat, and she hated sleeping, because of the nightmares.

Dr. Brown's question lingered for a while. It was that very question she'd desperately wanted to be asked for a long time. But no one thought to ask her. It was also that question that may have kept her from hurting herself. She knew that her family would never ask because they didn't want her to face the pain head on. They were never good at dealing with pain and working through it.

"Thank you for asking me," Reneata said before folding over into a heart-wrenching cry that echoed through the office. Startled, Dr. Brown quickly rose from his chair and raced to her side. But he stopped, just before embracing her, to let her cry.

Watching Reneata at her most vulnerable state, he realized that the young woman sitting before him was not a warrior. Nor was she a ruthless drug dealer. Instead she was a troubled soul who only wanted to be heard.

When he finally reached for her hand, she grabbed him by the waist, tucked her head into his stomach and continued to cry until there were no more tears left.

"All my life it's been about someone else. Not me. And I'm not trying to be a victim. I've just wanted everyone to know that what I feel matters."

"I understand, but you still haven't told me. How did all of this make you feel?"

Reneata wiped the tears from her face. "She was never there for me. And then she was. First, she took us away from Gramps and Ervin and all our friends to live with Brad. To protect me. Then, on the day I tried to hurt myself, there she was again trying to be a real mom. She saved my life. But in 19 days, I haven't heard from her. I don't want a mom that shows up sometimes, I need her all the time – everyday. But that's not how it works between us and I don't know why."

Dr. Brown squeezed her hands. There was so much more about the incident that Reneata didn't know. Dr. Brown had nuggets of information about her relationship with her mother. Things he'd learned from her grandfather and her sister. He also knew about what happened during the days leading to her suicide attempt, but he was unable to share any of this information. It caused him to feel like a fraud because he couldn't help her more.

"I have some good news," Dr. Brown finally said while staring at their hands entangled in a firm grip. "You are going home a few days early. Your grandfather insists that you are ready, and your doctors agree."

"Thank God!" she cried.

Dr. Brown returned to his desk and began shuffling papers to avoid looking her way.

"You are disappointed?" she asked, puzzled.

"You're not ready."

"Stop using me as a case study. This is my life!" she cried, and a nurse poked her head in the door to make sure everything was okay.

After reassuring the nurse that everything was fine, Dr. Brown finally looked at Reneata, shaking his head in disappointment. "I would never use you, Reneata, but you have more to deal with, more to overcome. I've listened to your story. You've been through so much, but there's more, I know it. You still don't remember what happened to you, do you?"

A bit unnerved, she sat motionless for a while before shaking her head, no. "I don't remember anything about my attempted suicide. I don't know why, but I don't remember enough to make sense of why I wanted to hurt myself so violently."

"I didn't think so."

"But regardless, I need my life back," she insisted. "I deserve this. I did everything you asked of me."

"And you believe your ex-boyfriend killed your brother as revenge for something you did nine years before. And what are the rest of us supposed to believe about you? How will all of this impact the rest of your life?" Dr. Brown said.

"Maybe I'm wrong. I don't know. Even if the real killers are never caught, I promise not to let this define my life, trust me. I won't let it."

Dr. Brown stood from his desk, walked to where Reneata was standing, then kissed her on the forehead. He called the red-haired nurse into his office to escort Reneata to her room for the last time. Reneata met the nurse at the door, looked back toward Dr. Brown, who had returned to his desk and a pile of paperwork without looking her way again.

Later that day, he came to her room to say goodbye.

"Against everything I've ever learned in this profession, the short time I've been in it, I am giving you this. Use it, if or when, you need a friend." When he was certain the nurse wasn't looking, he stuck his business card with a number written on the back in Reneata's hand.

Without looking down at the card; Reneata slid it into the pocket of her bag and gave him a big hug.

"Do you mind if we pray before you leave?" Surprised, Reneata took his hand. He had been a great friend to her, and she wanted to leave things right between them. Dr. Brown had unknowingly given her a second chance, and she loved him for that.

CHAPTER 14: LONG KISS GOODNIGHT

One Month Later

The stuffy bus reeked of urine and sweat. Reneata's bag, tucked under the seat in front of her, had so few things in it she wondered why she'd packed at all. Three pairs of panties, a pair of jeans, a tank top and one thin sweater stuffed underneath a waddled white lacy handkerchief that stored the engagement ring Ty had given her.

Her seatmate, a young boy cradling a blue and white blanket in his arms, slept soundly as the bus hissed and bumped along the highway. The young boy's mother, who sat across from them, leaned in his direction to ensure he was sleeping comfortably. She smiled at Reneata, who tried to smile back as often as she could. That sweet mother's smile was good to her. Her bloodshot eyes were a glimpse of what she felt inside, and mustering a smile - although just for a second – broke through the sadness.

"You alright?" the young mother finally asked.

Reneata nodded her head with the same energy the old deacons exhibited when you approached them to leave the church before the benediction. There was no way in hell those deacons would let you out those doors, and there was no way in hell Reneata could be anything less than okay to a stranger at that very moment. What was she to say? Weeks in a crazy hospital, trying to remember what she needed to forget. Ervin was gone. Her momma hated her. Her little sister was left to figure it out on her own. And the one man she loved most, left to live the life they planned together without her. And now she was leaving it all behind, like a coward, running away to avoid facing the truth.

Reneata stayed awake long enough to know the bus had crossed the Georgia state line. The finish line of her life as Reneata Morris. She was starting over, but this time as Reneata Tate. Reneata Denise Tate, twenty-four, smart, shy, and unassuming. Ambitious, harmless and without a past. She was becoming new again. She was taking her second chance.

Just past 3 a.m. when the bus pulled into the station, everyone, including the young boy, sluggishly walked out of the station doors and onto the Atlanta city street where someone was waiting to take them home.

"What is this?" Gene whispered in Reneata's ear as she fell into her arms just moments after saying hello. It wasn't Reneata's style to be vulnerable, but whenever she needed to be, her once best friend, Gene, was always there.

Draped in an orange sweater covering an African print t-shirt, a black skirt, brown tights, and black boots, Gene looked exactly how Reneata remembered her. Her long braids tied to the top of her head with a Kente cloth, and her earlobes pulled slighted towards her shoulders from her tarnished Nefertiti earrings.

"Get her bag," Gene instructed, with the whip of her hand, and a slender guy who was only one step off the heel of her shoes immediately picked up Reneata's limp satchel and headed towards the car. He wore an odd pair of blue-rimmed glasses, matching denim jeans and jacket, and old school Converse sneakers. Reneata later learned that the guy was Gene's new beau, Derrick.

Although it was Reneata's first time meeting him, she'd heard nothing but nice things about him from Ms. T, Gene's grandmother. He was who Reneata wanted for her friend – conservative, modestly good looking, and smart. But Reneata had to be honest with herself, she'd never imagined Gene being with a black guy. Gene had had a thing for white boys when they were in high school. Although there were no white guys in their old neighborhood, Gene spent most of her time tutoring kids two cities away from Tinsley, and that was where she fell head over heels for the first of many white boys she'd date throughout high school.

"Thought I was all cried out," Reneata admitted, as an excuse for falling into Gene's arms.

"No such thing," Gene assured her, and smiled while gently hugging the shoulder of her tired friend while walking to the car.

It felt like there had been no pause in the girls' friendship. As if the last two years, when they didn't speak, had not happened. Gene was there for Reneata now, the same way she was there when she became Reneata's friend at thirteen-years-old. They met one day when Gene approached Reneata in the girl's bathroom at school. Reneata was crying in an unlocked bathroom stall. She'd recently discovered she was pregnant with Byron's baby and she had no idea what to do. Gene, who was wise beyond her years, told Reneata that no matter what she did – have the baby or not – she would be okay, but what she decided to do needed to be the best decision for her and the baby, and not for Byron.

Tossed around from relative to relative while her mother tried to kick a bad drug habit, Gene was left to live with her grandmother when she was nine-years-old. They lived in a two-bedroom apartment down from Reneata and her family in C-Way. They didn't have much, but Ms. T did her best to make sure her only granddaughter had all she needed to have a good life. Gene was one of the smartest girls in their class, but unlike Reneata, she was more ambitious and driven.

From the day they met, they never left each other's side except the year JoAnn moved the girls to live with Brad, and when Gene left for college two years ago. Reneata was jealous and heartbroken to see her go, although she could have pursued college as well. The separation drove a wedge in their friendship, or so Reneata thought. But all she had to say was 'Ervin is dead' and Gene had wired her the cash to travel and promised her a safe place to live for as long as she needed.

For the next few months, Reneata was engulfed in a new world. Derrick became like a brother to her, and Gene did what Reneata knew she would do - held it together, refused to let Ervin's death tear her apart, and gave her another chance to beat the weariness.

"School?" Reneata snorted, one day as she and Gene ate bagels at the dining room table in her studio apartment. Her place was above a candy factory in a rather rough side of Atlanta. The space had never been intended to house people, only boxes and equipment, but Gene made it work.

"Girl, you'll do well in school. Have you thought about it?"

"I used to, but I don't anymore. No one cares if I go to school. Streets taught me plenty, plus I thought you would home school me. Smartest person I know and all."

Gene took the off-brand cream cheese, spread it over the cinnamon raisin bagels Derrick had picked up at Sando's Bakery earlier that morning, and covered the cheese in syrup. Licking the running syrup from the side of the bagel, she gave Reneata a slight smile. "Seriously. What can I teach you that you don't already know? You would do well in school, Re. You already smart and you would like the way it feels."

"The way it feels?" she snickered. "You talkin' like it's a long kiss goodnight. It's school – classes, grades, teachers, and people trying too hard. That's not my scene."

"Just come to class with me a few days and let me know what you think. I promise you'll like it."

"Don't they take attendance?" Reneata asked, nibbling at

the toasted edge of the bagel. Crumbs collected on the side of her plate. She brushed them to the floor, then watched as Gene's slight smile turned into a frown at her blatant disregard for the small, but always tidy, kitchen.

"Not all of them. I have a few in lecture halls. Economics and Ethics. No one takes attendance until we have an exam. We can sit in the back, and if you don't like it, leave. Nobody will care."

"I'll think about," Reneata said, unsure, and a bit uncomfortable with her friend's request. School was a sore spot for her since the day she turned down three academic scholarships during her senior year of high school. She remembered, Tinsley High School principal, Ms. Atwell, calling JoAnn and Gramps to her office for a meeting to discuss Reneata's future. JoAnn showed up half-high and mad as hell that she had to leave work. All it took was for Ms. Atwell to insinuate that Reneata's decision to stay in Tinsley and help her family put food on the table was a bad idea, and JoAnn lit into her like a raging bull trapped in a closet. JoAnn called the woman every piece of shit, snotty SOB ever imagined. Ervin was to go to school, but that didn't happen. The next was Tess, but for Reneata, she was to stay close, meet a half-decent guy, and help JoAnn navigate the crummy life she'd created.

"What are you studying anyway? You still want to be an attorney?"

"Of course," Gene smiled. "You are looking at the first sister on the Supreme Court, right here." Gene pointed her index finger square in the center of her chest.

"Right out of C-Way," Reneata added, and they both laughed.

"A black superhero. You remember that, Re? Me and you, the Wonder Twins from the League of Justice," Gene giggled.

"Oh, I remember," Reneata snickered. "If anybody can do

it, you can. You were always smart and crazy fearless. But that's not me. I'm still trying to understand back home. Get myself together. School can't fix what's wrong."

"Why are you blaming yourself? Ervin had problems and possibly enemies. What's that got to do with you?"

"You got all this, Gene," Reneata said, waving her hand in the air like Vanna White. "And I got the past. You, better than anybody, know what I did. Let's not pretend like it all started the day Ervin died."

"Yea, right," Gene said sarcastically. "This all started the day you shot heroin in Ervin's arm, just like my mom. He killed his own dreams. You didn't cause that. Did you make mistakes? Hell yea. Byron and the baby, but we got to carry our own cross and you've paid plenty already."

"Yea. Well. I wish that was all," Reneata said, still nibbling on the bagel.

"What you mean? Ervin's death, that's what this is all about, right?"

"I guess, I mean…"

"What? What is it?"

"I don't know," Reneata admitted. "It's about so many things. I mean -- I feel hollow in the inside, like I'm missing something that I'm being forced to live without. And it's not Ervin."

"Maybe it's your family. Maybe it's Ty. He loves you, Reneata."

"No. That's over," she insisted. She hadn't seen or talked to Ty in over six months. She'd heard rumors about how hard he was taking their breakup. He tried visiting her many times at Gramps's place after he returned from basic training, but she refused to see him. It was best they went their separate ways.

"It's been six months, and all you do is sit around this house, talk to some random dude on the phone, and club-hop. No different than what you did back home before I left. All that potential wasted because you are afraid," Gene said. "Just come to class with me a couple of times and then make up your mind."

"About what? I can't afford to go to the school."

"Hell! I can't afford it either. Not the point. Get inspired, then get off my couch and do something," Gene insisted.

"For you, Ms. Gene. I'm there. But don't be disappointed."

For the next several months, Reneata attended class with Gene one day a week. She blended in so well, she began to make friends and often joined them for study group and coffee dates in the mornings. It was like a long kiss goodnight, just as Gene had said.

One Year in Atlanta

Gene politely kicked Reneata out a few weeks before her graduation. She said it was time for her to fly, even if she felt her wings hadn't completely healed.

As expected, Derrick proposed marriage to Gene, and they started planning their wedding. She got accepted to law school and Derrick started a new job working in finance.

For the next year, Reneata slept on the couches of friends she'd met while attending class with Gene. She took a job book-keeping at a medical supply company and worked as a bartender at a local strip club on the weekends to save money for school.

Eventually, she met a man. Kwame. He owned the strip club and a few small businesses throughout the south. He thought she was pretty, and he paid to have her at his beck and call when he needed the attention of a woman. After two dates and three late night, early morning hookups, he surprised her with an apartment in the city. He never asked about her past or expected much from her other than to be there when he stopped by and to never call his house or his cellphone after 6 p.m.

Kwame had this indecent macho-ness that was forced and awkward. Short in comparison to any man she'd ever thought of dating, his clumsiness in bed made him that much more unintimidating. But he needed to feel like 'The Man' and Reneata knew all too well how to do that.

She never thought she could date a man for money. Although, Byron had set a high standard that was hard for any man to compete with. Ty had been a hard worker who never let the week come to an end without taking her out to a nice restaurant or buying her a bouquet of flowers. Kwame had a little bit of all of that. But he also had this demanding manner that left her feeling unappreciated when he was around. He was the type of guy who wrapped himself (and his ego) in a $2,000 suit, a gold Rolex, and a pocket stuffed with cash, every time he left the house.

"You are really dating a guy named, Kwame," Gene giggled.

"Come on. That's not cool," Reneata said, and they both laughed. Victor's Bar and Grill near Buckhead was their meetup spot once a month.

"What's so good about this Kwame guy that you can't finish school?" Gene asked, after the bartender slid their strawberry daiquiris across the bar and they walked back to their high-top table.

"That's the thing. I did finish. Kwame put me in a little place in the city, and I took classes online."

"What!" Gene jumped from the bar chair then ran to Reneata's side to gave her a big congratulatory hug. "I'm so proud of you," she cried.

"Sis. Good for you," Derrick added, a bit startled by Gene's sudden jolt from the chair.

"Good? Don't you mean great?" Gene said. "My girl is doing it!"

"Calm down," Reneata laughed. "It's only an associate degree."

"We don't care if it's a certificate in brick masonry. You are making lemonade, and that's what it's all about."

When Gene and Derrick left the bar, Reneata met some friends at a club and celebrated graduating from school. Gene made her feel so accomplished, although she was clueless about what she wanted to do next.

When Reneata returned home, just past 3 a.m., she had a visitor waiting outside her apartment door.

"Gramps! Is that really you?" she said, stumbling towards him with her purse in one hand and a pair of stockings crumbled in her other hand.

"You look beautiful, baby girl," Gramps said, hugging her tightly, despite the overpowering smell of men's cologne that hung from her body like a noose.

Gramps sat quietly at her kitchen table, waiting for her to shower and sober up. He overlooked her nasty apartment and the stink of molded Chinese food on the counter. Instead, he sat and talked to her like nothing had happened.

"Everyone, especially me, misses you. Ty. JoAnn, and your little sister."

"I've only been gone a little over a year."

"We know, but it's not the same back home and I'm worried about you."

"No need to. I'm fine."

"Okay," he said, unconvinced. "Why not come home? Things have gotten better."

"I'm not ready," she said, feeling guilty he'd driven all the way to see her, to return alone.

"I had a feeling you would say that."

"Don't get me wrong, I miss you," she said. "But there's nothing for me there... Did they," Reneata started to speak, but stopped.

"Did they catch the killer?" he finished for her. "No. No word. No progress. We are trying not to give up, but also trying not to let it bury us."

"I understand."

"I didn't come here to talk about that. I wanted to see my granddaughter. Make sure she's eating and happy and prayed for."

"Well. Did I pass the test?"

Gramps looked around the apartment, then shook his head, yes.

"Good," she said, knowing he was lying.

"I had a feeling you wouldn't return home with me but I wanted to tell you face-to-face that when you are ready, we want you back where you belong."

"I know, but this is my home now."

Gramps smiled. "I said years ago that you could make a home anywhere. You were my Rambler. Remember that?"

"Of course," she smiled. "You see an adventurer in me, but I don't know."

"You know," Gramps said confidently.

They talked for more than an hour before he left for his three-hour ride back to Tinsley.

One week later, Reneata received a letter from Gramps, thanking her for welcoming him into her home and asking her for one favor – to remain his Rambler.

The following week, Reneata received a second letter from Gramps. But unlike the first one, it was taped on top of a small shoebox. The letter read, "Stay open and explore and when you are ready, return home, we miss you."

Reneata opened the box and found another envelope with a round-trip airline ticket to the Bahamas, a confirmation number for a resort on the beach, and three hundred dollars cash.

"What is this?" Reneata said with a smile in her voice when she called Gramps.

"Don't overthink it, Reneata. This is a gift from all of us. Have fun and we love you." Before Reneata could respond, Gramps hung up the phone.

Reneata tucked the money and airline ticket under her mattress and tried not to give any thought to Gramps's generous gift. She didn't need a trip, she wasn't into travelling on her own, not now. Maybe never.

CHAPTER 15: FINDING PEACE

18 Months in Atlanta

Fifteen after two and it was all over. Thirteen minutes after it started. Two minutes after the pinching from his blue jean zipper stopped tugging at the inside of her thigh. This new guy, Ced, didn't even take his pants off. Reneata lay flat on her back the entire time, trying to think of something soft and fluffy instead of hard and jagged.

He rolled over onto his side, pulled his pants up in an awkward jerk, and buckled them in place, all while she tugged the white sheets just above the top of her breasts. She felt puny, like the first day after flu symptoms dissipated. Stale and stool brown. Nothing was new or brilliantly bright, as she'd hoped. No birds were singing sweet lullabies or dandelions blowing in the wind. Instead, her pink bandage-tight dress was entangled around her left leg, and to suit, when Ced rolled off the side of the bed, he snatched the sheet, then chuckled neurotically as she scrambled to cover her naked body.

"Cold?" he asked, while gathering his things. He didn't wait for Reneata to answer before heading towards the bathroom door. By the time she tried to respond, he'd slammed the door behind him.

Reneata and Kwame had stopped seeing each after his wife found out about their relationship and the apartment. He stopped coming by, and the rent was now hers to handle alone. She called herself getting back out there and meeting someone new. But this guy was far from what she needed – it didn't take long for her to see that.

Seconds after the faucet shut off, she smelled the stinging scent of a freshly lit cigarette. After hearing him snicker, she realized Ced was talking to someone on a cell phone.

"Yea, man, got it," he said. "Naw, she ain't all that. Nothing to it, you know how I do."

What the hell? she thought, before wiggling feverishly to get her dress back in place. She was cold. Chill bumps quickly covering her legs and arms and the damp air made the buzz from the liquor dissipate.

Ced stood in the bathroom doorway and watched Reneata with the same look of conceit and pity that Byron had on his face the first time they had sex.

"You chilly?" Ced asked with his fingers clutched around the remaining half of his cigarette.

"Yep. Cold and ready to go." Reneata stood to find her shoes.

"You don't have to leave. Just get the cover," he said, but she ignored him and kept looking for her things. Realizing that one of her shoes was tangled in the sheets, she sat on the side of the bed and searched through the pile of covers while Ced continued to watch her. But just when she thought she had the shoe, Ced snatched the cover, then watched as she rolled off the bed, falling flat on her face.

"Silly ass girl, get up!" he snorted.

Reneata rolled to her knees and wrestled herself to her feet. Her strapless dress fell back below her bra-line. When she stood up, she covered her breasts with one hand and examined her face for scratches, blood, and carpet burns with the other. Ced threw the cover at her, then laughed like she was a clown at the circus.

The ride home was the longest ride she'd had in a long time. Reneata sat next to Ced, someone who didn't give a damn about her, while thinking that Ty was elsewhere in the world, living the life they had promised to share together. She stared out of the car window in a fog of despair. She'd sought companionship in the dingy sheets of a cheap hotel room. Desperately in need of a warm body to cradle next to. But all she had found was more loneliness.

Ced dropped Reneata off, then sped from the parking lot without ensuring she made it in her apartment safely. She stood watching as his car taillights faded into the night. A sick and shameful feeling grew in the pit of her stomach. This was what her life had come to – another bad relationship, another careless affair. Dr. Brown was right all along, she wasn't ready. Nothing had changed except her zip code, and it wasn't enough to give her the peace she longed for. It was time to do the hard work; to stop looking for love from someone else and start learning to love herself.

Four days later, Reneata was on a flight to the Bahamas. She was finally ready to see if she could be the adventurer Gramps always thought she was.

The sun appeared above the palm tree's tall brushes in a fuss of clouds. Reneata moved from cabana to cabana, thinking she could feel the sun more directly if she found the perfect spot. But the rays weren't consistent, instead they strayed in all directions, making the wind that blew through her hair mild and cool. When the sun settled behind the clouds, the sound of the ocean was louder. But when the clouds disappeared, the sun filled the beach with joy.

It was all new to her, watching the sun play peek-a-boo in the clouds, existing with nowhere to go, and feeling the ocean breeze on her face. She was alone, but she didn't feel alone at all. Especially when a lively flock of seagulls paraded just above her cabana, and the warm sand covered her feet. Instead she felt at home, as if she were always meant to be there.

"Ma'am, can I get you anything?" A short woman with dreadlocks and a big bright smile approached the cabana with a menu in her hand.

"Like what?" Reneata asked, trying not to sound like it was her first time on the beach.

"We can make any drink you like, or water, or soda."

"Oh. Okay. Water sounds great for now."

"Maybe a specialty drink from the bar later? We have amazing Pina Colada."

"Maybe. But I didn't bring my purse. I'll need to go back to my room."

"No need," the waitress smiled. "Everything comes in your all-inclusive package. You are our special guest. Order what you like, it's already taken care of."

"I didn't know that," she said. "This trip is a gift from my grandfather."

"Well, he really loves you," the waitress replied, and Reneata smiled from ear to ear.

For the next four days, she basked in the sunshine, built sandcastles near the shore, slept peacefully in her cabana, and enjoyed the company of other resort guests who treated her like family.

She met a couple from New Zealand who'd never visited the U.S. but had dreamed of seeing New York City. She met a father and his daughter from Costa Rica, who was in the Bahamas celebrating the daughter's 15th birthday; and a widow who'd recently buried her husband of 30 years who had decided to return to the place where they met to scatter his ashes in the ocean.

No one thought it was strange that she was alone, or questioned her intentions or her past, instead they shared a cocktail at the hotel's bar and played checkers by the pool. They shared stories about their travels and invited Reneata to join them for dinner. She had never felt so at peace in a place unlike her home. She truly was a rambler, as Gramps often said. She'd found her four-leaf clover.

Upon returning to Atlanta when her vacation was over, Reneata found a package at her door. It was from her mother, to whom she'd spoken only once since leaving Tinsley over a year ago. When she opened the package, she found a new bathing suit and a note.

"Sorry, I didn't get this to you sooner but I'm sure you will need it for the next time."

Next time, Reneata thought. *What did that mean?*

The trip to the Bahamas had to have cost Gramps more than a thousand dollars, maybe his entire retirement and social security check for the month. Reneata knew she couldn't afford a trip like that on what she made as a bookkeeper and bartender at the club. This had been a once in a lifetime opportunity and she was grateful for it, but she didn't expect anything more from him. She knew Gramps wanted her to have a big life. To see the world and explore it on her own terms. He had respected what Ty was trying to give her, but he wanted Reneata to have these experiences for herself. So, it was no surprise when the second envelope arrived with a round-trip airline ticket, a stack of twenty-dollar bills, and a note that simply said, "Go!"

CHAPTER 16: PINK SAND

Stanley stood outside the airport arrival area, twirling a sign with Reneata's misspelled name written on it. When she saw it, she smiled, then walked up to him and said, "I think that's me."

"You are Miss Reneeta, I suppose?" Stanley said, looking her squarely in the eyes.

"I am Miss Reneata," she snickered. "But it's no problem."

"So sorry, Miss Reneata," he said, in a beautiful British accent that seemed out of sync coming from a man as dark as the sky against a crescent moon night.

He kissed the center of her hand before grabbing her bags and hurriedly placing them in the back of the car.

Reneata smiled awkwardly when he kissed her. It was a strange gesture, but he was friendly, and she wasn't sure if hand-kissing was a traditional greeting in Bermuda, so, she took it for what it was worth.

"First time in Bermuda?"

"Yes."

"Well, let's get you to your room so you can enjoy the pink sand beaches."

"Pink beaches? Really?"

"Well, of course," he said, while opening her car door.

The airport was filled with vacationers, but there were only a few cars on the street. "There are many things we do not have here that you may enjoy, like Walmart and McDonalds, but we do have the most beautiful beaches in the world. And just think ... all you had to do was cross over the Bermuda triangle to get here," he laughed.

"So true," she smiled.

While they rode through the city, Stanley told Reneata about the island's history, the beaches and golfing and the unique way Bermudian's lived. She'd had no idea it was British territory and the entire island was less than 30 miles long. She knew nothing about Bermuda and had been a bit hesitant to take the trip because it felt different from going to a popular tourist attraction like the Bahamas.

After a short drive, Stanley stopped the car in front of a turquoise-colored residential home with an oddly designed white rooftop. Reneata stepped out of the car and stood to look at the house in awe.

"The roofs here are made of limestone and are used to collect the island's water supply. We gather the rainwater stored in tanks inside or near the house. Also, the limestone keeps indoors cool."

"Wow. I've never seen anything like it. Very eco-friendly."

"We are, as you say, 'very eco-friendly' here," he smiled.

"And these colors. It looks like candy-land," Reneata admired.

"Our landscape symbolizes who we are as a people. It reflects Bermudian's positive outlook on life."

"I love it," Reneata said while walking towards the house. When she reached the porch, she looked back at the beautiful stone walkway, and smiled again, but this time at Stanley, who was struggling to get her luggage up the stairway.

"Let me help you," she said, but he shook his head, no, then fought to get the bags up the steps and into the house.

"You will love it here, Miss Reneata. Tourists aren't allowed to drive cars, but you can drive a motor scooter. There are several in the back. If you need to get somewhere far, I can drive you."

"You live here?" Reneata asked.

"Yes. Me and my sister, Shirlee. But no worries, you will have a wing of the house to yourself. Your own bedroom, bath, and patio that overlook the ocean. We will prepare your meals and you are welcome to join us in the common areas of the house whenever you like."

"Wow. Okay. If you don't mind me asking, how do you know my grandfather?"

Stanley continued getting her things on the porch before answering her question. She knew he was stalling but she wasn't sure why.

"I knew your brother, Ervin," he finally answered.

Surprised, Reneata suddenly stopped, then turned in Stanley's direction. "What? How?"

"We met at an Art Institute in Boston when we were only lads. He was the most outstanding sculptor I ever met. I was there because of my drawings, and we became friends."

"I'd never heard of you - I didn't know."

"There is no reason for you to be sorry. Your brother spoke of you often – his little sis with the big smile and long ponytails who loved dollhouses. I hadn't spoken to Ervin in years when I heard of his death. I wrote your mother and grandfather to give them my condolences and, in the letter, I mentioned that I owned a bed and breakfast in Bermuda and offered to host them if they ever wanted to come here."

"So, they sent me?" Reneata said with a swell of tears in her eyes.

"They said 'to treat you like royalty'. I plan to make them

proud."

Reneata hugged Stanley unexpectedly and thanked him. She was overwhelmed at the thought that he had spent time with Ervin before he started using drugs. She felt connected to him in some way because he knew how great Ervin really was. That meant a lot to her.

For the next week, she explored the island, drank virgin daiquiris on her personal patio, learned to play golf at one of the most exclusive hotels on the island and experienced the most delicious Bermudian meals ever. Stanley accompanied her when he could, and his sister Ms. Shirlee treated her like royalty, just as Stanley promised. She was more relaxed in Bermuda than any place she'd ever been.

"Only one more day left," Stanley said, while eating breakfast with Reneata and Ms. Shirlee on the morning of Reneata's last day on the island. "Have you enjoyed yourself?"

"No," Reneata said with a smile in her voice.

"What?" he replied. "You kidding me, right? I saw you parasailing yesterday, screaming from the top of your lungs and laughing all at the same time. And don't forget the traffic scuffle you caused on that motor scooter that had everyone pointing and laughing at you."

"I had a great time," Reneata said to everyone's delight. "This has been the most amazing trip. I adore how you live. It's so peaceful here, and calm. No traffic jams – except the one I caused, of course – no high demands, nothing. It has been amazing. Thank you so much."

"That's it," Stanley said. "Just thank you?"

"Well, yes. What more do you want?"

"Honestly?" he asked, curiously smiling at his sister. "You owe me a dance. Tonight. At our annual summer festival in the Parish. It starts at 6 p.m., are you game?"

"Of course, I am, but I can't dance, so don't expect too much."

"Bull. I've never met a black girl from the States who couldn't dance. We will see later."

At 6 p.m. sharp, Stanley, dressed in all white linen, and Reneata, in a pink halter dress, walked arm-in-arm into the Summer Fest, and for the next two hours they danced under the moonlight as if no one else was on the dance floor but them.

Swirling into Stanley's arms and laughing so loud she could hear herself over the blasting music, Reneata felt this internal joy that clicked on like a light switch. She'd found it again, somewhere new. She felt the purpose of her journey – she began to understand why Gramps and the rest of the family wanted her to experience something more. Beyond the Alabama sky, there was a world filled with beauty and adventure, and she was ready to see it all.

Stanley and Reneata walked hand-in-hand back to the bed and breakfast, laughing and talking all the way. When they reached the door to her room, Stanley gently grabbed her shoulders to pull her closer for a kiss. Reneata, who thought the world of Stanley, and had no intention of hurting his feelings, slowly moved from his embrace.

"I'm sorry," he said, confused by her actions. "I just thought. Well, I thought you liked me."

Smiling from ear to ear, Reneata nodded her head in agreement, then took his hands. "I came here to find myself. If I let this happen, then my journey becomes more about you than me. I need this to remain my journey. I hope you understand."

Stanley smiled back at her before kissing her hand. "No need to ever explain to me or anyone else about the desires of your heart. Love starts with you first. The rest will fall in line."

"Thank you," she said before giving him a big friendly

embrace.

Before going to bed on her last night on the island, Reneata fell to her knees to pray. She thanked God for the trip, her family, Stanley, Ms. Shirlee, and for another chance at life. The next morning, she said goodbye to Stanley and Ms. Shirlee and promised to stay in touch.

"Gramps, you should have seen me parasailing, it was crazy. I can't thank you enough, it's been amazing."

"Sweetheart, we are so happy for you. But please, don't just thank me. This is a gift from everyone - me, JoAnn, Tess, and even a few of my buddies at the community center, they all pitched in. We just want you to enjoy yourself."

"I can't believe it. I just thought it was from you and maybe the family. But other people helped, your friends helped? I'm so grateful. Thank you."

"Never a problem, baby, we love you. But what's next? We can give you a few dollars towards another trip…."

"No. I won't take it this time. I will pay for my next trip on my own. I hope you understand?"

"Yes, I do," Gramps smiled.

"I have a plan. I have decided to leave my job at the medical supply company and go to work at a local nonprofit in the area that's looking for an experienced bookkeeper."

"Is the pay better?"

"Somewhat. But most importantly, I can travel with the nonprofit. They do missionary work in the U.S. and abroad, and I can go, help them serve the community and see the world."

"Sweetheart that sounds amazing," Gramps said. "Where to first?"

"We are heading to New Orleans to help with clean-up after the hurricane. If we stop off in Birmingham, I promise to call you."

"Please do. Everyone wants to see you."

For the next two years, Reneata worked and traveled to places she never thought she'd ever see. She went to Burundi, Africa to help provide healthcare to the community; Sierra Leone to feed the hungry, and she spent time in La Paz, Bolivia as a service-aid to the nonprofit's executive director. And when she wasn't traveling for work, she would steal away in the Caribbean, spending her downtime on the beach. Her life had evolved, but she was still missing the one thing she wanted most. Love.

After a tough mission trip to the Congo, Reneata returned to Atlanta, quit her job at the nonprofit, and decided to return to school to earn her bachelor's degree. She picked up a few hours bartending at the Girl Haven Strip Club, the same club she had worked at years before. She decided it was time to take what she'd learned during her trips, and either, write a book, or use her knowledge to find a good-paying job.

She still hadn't returned to Alabama to see her family, but she spoke with them often, and knew they supported her in everything she did. She'd made a promise to herself that she would make it home by her 30th birthday, which was less than 18 months away.

CHAPTER 17: CORY

2009 - 4 Years in Atlanta

Cory Debose was the fourth person in-line at Bistro Coffeehouse in the city. Talking on his cell phone, he occasionally smiled, as if the universe belonged to him and the rest of the world was anxious wanna-bes. Too clean-cut and handsome to be an actor or a musician, and too suave to be a dope boy, he was exactly the type of guy Reneata never thought she could have.

His dark gray, European-cut, pinstriped pants complimented his brown Italian loafers in an odd, out of sync fashion. The same way a petite rich girl could wear polka dots with stripes, but a fat, broke girl couldn't.

His distinctiveness was about more than what he wore; he was by far the only human left in a graveyard filled with late night/early morning zombies - clubbers still recovering from the double shot of cheap liquor they drank just before the last call. Unfortunately, Reneata was one of them. That night, after losing a bet with the strip club owner, Sam, she'd voyaged onto the stage for the first time. Twirling her glitter-covered naked body in a row of more experienced dancers, she planted a big fake smile on her face, then gave the men what they wanted. A hundred hands touched her body while her too tight, feathered getup tore welts onto her thighs and underarms. The pain was yet another remnant from her meager career choice. All she wanted to do was travel and experience things she never thought were possible, but the despair she witnessed while wrapping up her last missionary trip caused the pain, which she'd thought she'd left Alabama to get away from, to resurface. She wasn't sleeping. Instead, she lay in bed thinking about her family and Ty.

For as much as she pretended to hate the idea of getting on that stage, she needed the money. When she left the nonprofit, she had no clue how much money she'd saved by traveling and eating at the charity's expense. It had been more than a job with half-decent pay; it was a second home to her, and she missed it.

Just before her first lap dance came to an end, some guy spilled vodka and orange juice in Reneata's hair. Big Bobby, Girl Haven's bouncer, dragged the sloppy drunk man from the club by his tattooed arm. Reneata, now even more embarrassed than before, ran to the dressing room to clean up and clock out. The club was closing, she was a little tipsy and ready to clean the night off her body.

Tossing her feathered costume in the trash, she combed her damp hair into a ponytail, threw on some lip-gloss, jeans, and a pink Polo shirt, and left the club looking more like a sorority girl than an amateur dancer.

Now, she stood in line with the others, trying to sober up before making the half-mile walk to her apartment. Her jean pockets were bursting with dollar bills, which brought her more attention from the coffeehouse patrons than she wanted. She grabbed an empty Bistro Coffeehouse paper bag from a table and dumped the money into it when no one was looking. One of the other zombies recognized her from the club and started her way. Reneata bee-lined towards the counter, broke in front of a guy who couldn't decide between black coffee and a double shot energy drink, and placed her order. Just as she rushed past the indecisive patron, the well-dressed guy on his cellphone caught her eye.

"Hi," he said, awkwardly stepping one foot across the other like he was performing a curtsey. "My name is Cory." Pouring her third pack of sugar into the coffee cup, Reneata pretended not to hear him.

He patiently stood, waiting for her response while slowly stirring his tea.

"I'm sorry, are you talking to me?" Reneata asked arrogantly, now overloading her coffee with cream, and not because she liked cream, but because she needed a reason to stay at the counter.

Leaning forward to grab a pack of Splenda, his wide-frame blocked a few zombies from preparing their hot beverages - their last chance to sober up before work. It wasn't intentional; he was nervous, which intrigued Reneata.

"Yea, you, the pretty girl in the pink Polo," he said in a shaky tone with an infectious grin on his face.

"That's cute," she responded, spanning his tall, dark frame with her eyes before walking away from the counter. He followed her to the same empty high-top table where she'd snatched the coffeehouse bag to stash her tips just minutes before. She stared at him oddly when he took a seat across from her.

"Is this okay?" he asked, while scooting his stool closer to the table.

Reneata took the paper bag filled with money and rolled it as tight as she could, then stucked it under her thigh so that it wouldn't be a topic of discussion. He didn't notice anything.

"Do I know you?" she asked, knowing good and well she'd never seen him before.

"I don't know...do you? Ever been on the West Coast? Did you go to Pepperdine U. by chance? You do look familiar."

"So, you're at my table and you don't know me?" She blurted, "Don't you think that's odd?"

"Not really. The table belongs to the coffeehouse, and there is a reason they only have a few. They want us to get to know each other. Network. Nothing is by chance these days. This meeting will benefit you, the establishment, and me. Ever thought about it that way?"

She shrugged her shoulders and took a sip of coffee. He was rambling, and she wanted to stop him, but it was so cute she decided not to. His tone suggested a sense of pride because he thought he was teaching her something. She hated that feeling; when you meet someone new and they automatically believe you need to be schooled.

"Who is, 'they'?" she inquired sarcastically.

"The Bistro," he answered, still stirring his tea, which was now cold. "They planned 'this'; they single-handedly manipulated us into meeting each other by only having five tables and ten chairs. They wanted this to happen," he said flirtatiously.

"And what is 'this'?" Her tone was cynical, downright rude. She wanted him to think being hit on by a good-looking man was as common to her as taking a breath of fresh air.

When he heard the sarcasm in her voice, he stopped playing with his cold tea and gave her an awkward look she'd seen many times before. Typically, right before some jerk called her out her name.

"This is a chance of a lifetime," he quivered, obviously calling her bluff and trying to bring her down off the pedestal she'd placed herself on.

Shifting her head to show her haughtiness, Reneata rolled her eyes in his direction. "You've got to be kidding me, right? Is this how Pepperdine U. taught you to pick up a lady, by impressing her with your intellect and your conspiracy theories about coffee houses and then insulting her?"

"What makes you think I'm trying to pick you up?" he said, now no longer hiding behind the silly rules of first impressions. "Aren't you a little pretentious? It's eight in the morning; every man knows you should never pick up a woman before noon. It's bad luck."

She started to laugh. "You're kidding me, right?"

"Not at all. Think about it this way. It's eight a.m. on Friday morning. I'm dressed for work, along with most of the patrons here, and you are dressed for a day at the mall, but it's too early to shop. Nothing opens until ten a.m. If I had to guess, you are leaving some man's house, possibly your boyfriend's, maybe not. He either asked you to leave or threw you out, but not before you washed your hair with what smells like pineapple or coconut shampoo; painted on those jeans and headed out to find your next victim."

"Victim!" Reneata barked before leaping off the barstool. Twisting her ankle in the process, she spilled her coffee on the table, then jumped backward twice to avoid what she perceived would be third-degree burns from the hot coffee now rapidly rolling in her direction. The bag of money fell to the floor, leaving the base of the table covered with balled up dollar bills. Cory reached for the cup to keep the remaining coffee from escaping. Then he handed her a few napkins and tried to help her pick up the money from the floor, but she stopped him.

"Don't!" she shouted. The other zombies turned their heads toward her. Cory moved away slowly, with his hands in the air, like he was being boosted for armed robbery. Reneata finished picking up the money, then cleaned the coffee from the table while he sat in the corner, watching.

The owner of the Bistro came over to the table with a fresh cup of coffee, three sugars, and two creams, just as Reneata had prepared it before. She could hear Cory laughing from the corner. It felt like she was in her favorite episode of the *Twilight Zone*, *The Eye of the Beholder*. Cory was one of the pig face people and she was the ugly human.

"So, you're better now," he said, following her out the Bistro's door.

"Get away from me," she demanded, more ashamed than angry. He followed her for half a block, trying to apologize. But once he realized how pathetic he looked, chasing some girl down the street, he grabbed a cab and headed back to his hotel.

When Reneata turned to see where he was, he was gone. She breathed a sigh of relief. He was a lunatic, possibly a sociopath. JoAnn was right; there is nothing worse than a conceited man.

While her shower warmed, Reneata sat on the floor of her bedroom, thinking about *crazy* Cory and what he had said. She poured the money from the bag to count it, hoping it was enough to pay the light bill that month. In between a stack of bills was a business card. Convinced it was from one of the guys in the strip club, she began to rip it apart when she saw a handwritten message that said, 'There are no more beautiful things to love than a black woman'. When she turned the card over, she realized it belonged to Cory Dubose, the jerk from the coffeehouse.

Finding his business card, after their humiliating first encounter, was the best thing that had happened to Reneata in a long time. She called him a few days later, and they talked for hours. He apologized for insulting her, and she accepted his apology.

They had dinner once before he returned home to LA. They kept in touch for months after their first meeting. There was a lot they had in common, including the same taste in music, movies, and books. It didn't take long for Reneata to fall in love with Cory – but it felt different this time. Instead of expecting her to be the pretty girl on his side, he cared about her opinions. He asked about her goals, and best of all, he had no connection to her past.

Five months after they met, Corey flew her to LA to meet his father, Desmond Debose, an accountant; his mother, California State Senator Lucinda Debose; and his brother, James Debose, a pediatrician at a clinic in San Diego. It was the first time Reneata had been around wealthy black folks who weren't drug dealers and strip club owners.

When the plane landed in LA, she knew that once again her life was about to change. She'd quit bartending at the club and put her travel plans on hold. Her focus was to pursue her bachelors degree online and learn to assimilate into this new life with Cory, who wanted to marry her. She decided to give him a chance and to do two things she felt she had to do to move forward with her life – learn to let Cory love her and keep him from learning the truth about her past.

PART II: NIGHT

CHAPTER 18: SIX YEARS, NO ALABAMA

2012

"How you feel?" Cory asked, stroking the peach fuzz on his face. His gravelly voice startled Reneata, as she stood motionless under the steaming hot water. The bathroom filled with white fog just before he let in a rush of cool air from the bedroom.

"About what?" she yelled over the pouring shower. He'd asked that same question every day for the last week. Not 'how are you', but 'how you feel' - kind, but unlike him.

"Going home? First time in over five years, right?"

"Yep. I feel good. Why wouldn't I? Isn't home where the heart is?"

"Home is a person, and not a place," he said as Reneata wrapped a towel around her body and stepped out of the shower. "I like that better. Not so cliché."

He reached to kiss her, but she put her hand up to prevent his awful smelling shaving cream from getting on her face.

"No kissy-kissy today, momma?" he asked, sounding more like a kid than a thirty-five-year-old man.

"Are you ever serious?" Reneata smiled, thinking back on the corny guy with the brash personality she fell for at the Bistro Coffeehouse over a year ago.

"Yep," he said, and in one quick motion, he placed his hand on her lower back and gently pulled her wet body against his chest. "I'm serious in the boardroom, the bedroom, and the bank." With his strong arms wrapped around her, he intentionally smeared shaving cream on her nose while planting a big wet kiss just above her eyebrow.

Bravado filled the room like cigar smoke, and Reneata inhaled without hesitation. That was all it took to replace the edginess with a warm tingle directly in the center of her body. She giggled a bit until it passed, then playfully wiggled to break free. But her 5'10" frame had no chance of getting away from his 6'2" perfectly toned arms – so, she let it happen.

"Take that towel off," he whispered in her ear.

She shook her head, 'no' and smiled.

"Take that towel off," he pleaded again, low and sexy enough to raise chill bumps on her neck.

"No, Cory!" she shouted, pretending to stand her ground.

"You like to play hard to get?"

Swiveling her head back and popping her big brown eyes like a little girl vying for the last lollipop, she said, "You know me -- nothing comes easy."

He loved it...

"I'll let you go, but ten days is too long. Again. Explain to me why we're getting married in Alabama and not here in California, and why do I have to wait for my kisses?"

"You know the answer, stop kidding," she said.

"Oh. I remember. You want to make all your old boyfriends jealous."

"Something like that..." she chuckled.

"Be ready for me when I get there."

Reneata wiggled free from his arms and gave him a flirtatious nod, "Trust me, I will."

When the temperature in the room returned to normal, Cory started his usual slate of pre-wedding questions, just what Reneata wanted to avoid. It had taken her months to convince him to have their wedding down South. His mother hated the idea from the start but gave in when Reneata agreed to let Cory accompany her on an upcoming business trip to Africa. Of course, that meant Reneata would stay behind and limit her calls to once a day so his mother could have him all to herself. Reneata could see her now, strutting like a peacock on the dusty road of some downtrodden African village with her beautiful son at her side, and little African kids pulling at the hem of her dress. The perfect photo op: California Senator Dubose (all clad with a diamond tiara and magical stilettos) healing the sick and feeding the poor. She would be Diva of the Day. She didn't want any competition from anyone, especially her soon-to-be daughter-in-law whom she didn't particularly care for.

"What are your plans for the big A?" Cory asked while cleaning the razor for the second time before cautiously bringing it to his face for a close shave.

"The wedding. Tie up some loose ends. See some old friends...stuff like that."

"Plan to see Ty?"

If the goal was to catch her off guard, it worked, but she remained cool. "Why would I do that?"

Corey placed his razor in a cup filled with warm water and turned in her direction. "What do you mean, Reneata? He *was* the love of your life, right? You've told me that a million times. Your first... your 'hood' Knight in Shining Armor. Don't get it wrong, I'm corporate 'hood.' You get the best of both worlds...."

"Right," she blurted, if for no other reason than to shut him up and save him from himself.

Ty was a sore topic for the couple. Maybe because he was Reneata's first true love, or maybe because he was the only honest thing about her past that she'd shared with Cory, or anyone else, since arriving in California. She told Cory and his family that her brother, Ervin, a highly accomplished artist, had died in a tragic car accident, and her mother and grandfather raised Reneata and her younger sister, Tess, in a working-class family in a small town in Alabama. She never mentioned Ervin's drug addiction, his criminal record and murder, her guilt for what happened to him, the suicide attempt, or her time in the mental hospital.

The seriousness of Cory's face could not be missed. Reneata desperately needed to take an ax to the 800-pound gorilla in the room, so she started laughing, without merit, hoping to drown out his thoughts of Ty and shift the conversation to something less uncomfortable.

"Hood. Knight. Really, Cory? What son of a state senator with an Ivy League degree, a Puerto Rican 'nanna', and a trust fund big enough to feed a small country, knows about the 'hood', besides what he saw in *Boyz In The Hood*? No matter how big, black, and beautiful you are, sweetie, you would run every red light in Compton, in fear of your so-called 'hood' compadres."

Corey thought about it for a second, then chuckled. "When you're right, you're right," he conceded.

They dressed, and then met in the kitchen for their usual coffee and bagel.

Cory ran Heron Debose Marketing, an ad agency in LA, named after his great-grandfather, a famous artist and an advertising copywriter. Despite his mom's success, he had made a name for himself in that very competitive industry. He was an A-lister: the house they lived in was in an area often frequented by tour buses filled with people looking for movie star homes, and he was a member of the polo club and the country club. For good measure, he was also an affiliate of an imaginary club for black and wealthy folks in LA that Reneata often referred to as the "underground railroad society." Cory thought that was funny, and when he didn't want to tell her where he was going, he would say, "Its URS poker night," and beeline out the door. It was their little joke. Although she knew, if it did exist, the Dubose family, in some form or fashion, would chair the board.

The mornings were their only real time together. After long days at work, and after-hours political functions with his mom, Cory and Reneata's relationship was limited to bathroom flirtations and bagels. But she had signed on for it. And she loved him. Although she must admit, it wasn't that hang-off-the-rim-of-the-moon kind of love. It was a get-comfortable-in-your-favorite-old-chair kind of love - a quiet, and expected, kind of love. She was good with that. She'd had no expectations when they met, so finding him was like finding a diamond in shattered glass.

"You look beautiful this morning. Simple and beautiful," Cory said, as Reneata strolled into the kitchen, wearing his favorite tan jumpsuit and animal-print stilettos.

"Well, thank you," she responded in the worst Scarlett O'Hara impersonation she could conjure up.

He laughed, while raising his coffee cup, pretending to toast her humility. "Absolutely. That's what makes you stand out in this sea of fakeness in Cali. My girl can cook grits, speak fluent Ebonics with a hint of Southern charm, and wear the hell out of a Versace pants suit and Jimmy Choo's."

"Shut up, crazy!" she shot back at him, smiling. "You sound like a goof in love."

"Yep. One thing I learned from my dad years ago: before your girl goes away for a long trip without you, don't piss her off or make her feel nothing good is waiting for her when she returns. I know how cunning those Alabama *brotha's* can be, I got to get my game face on."

"Good move, you never know what I could get myself into," she said half-jokingly.

"Just don't get yourself into someone else's bed...." he said, and all the innocent humor was snatched from the room.

Reneata practically dropped her cup. "What? Where did that come from? Cory, look at me," she said as she tugged at the sleeve of his crisp, white, button-down. "I'm not going to rekindle the past. This trip is for us. It's time for me to go home and deal with what I left behind. I need to see what's left of my family; I need to see my friends." She rambled off everything she'd told herself for the last few weeks, but knew she wasn't doing a good job of convincing him because she still hadn't convinced herself. "We talked about this, and you told me you understood. Ten days, that's all, and then we'll get married there, and return to LA to live out our lives together, just as we planned. No worries, right?"

"What I know, is what you told me, Reneata. You have a sister you haven't seen, but she's not there anymore. Friends that never call you. You don't talk about your mom or grandfather, and your brother, well, he's gone. What's left in Alabama? If it's not Ty, what's there?"

"Really, Cory, this is how you send me off? Let me explain it to you this way: What's left is my past and our future. What's left is my life. You know everything. I've told you everything. Just trust me. Can you do that?"

"Right, no worries," he whispered while taking his now cold cup of coffee and pouring it down the drain.

Reneata had never seen him like that, but she had to admit, she liked it. JoAnn always told her to 'make sure he loves you more.' She'd had that with Ty, but she hadn't been ready then, and after what happened, she realized he might not have been the one. Cory was a different breed. He didn't need her. He was a big fish in LA, and she was not. She was riding his coattail. She didn't have the pedigree – an MBA from UCLA, or Harvard, or even a good story to tell about how she bootstrapped her way to the top, as most did in his circle of friends. She was just a young lady with a bad past, who got lucky by running into the right guy in a coffee house in Atlanta over a year ago.

Cory slammed the door behind him without saying good-bye - he didn't take his father's advice after all.

CHAPTER 19: GOING HOME

Hundreds of travelers scurried through LAX as Reneata finished her second bag of licorice. Cory hated to see her eating candy, especially in the morning, but her plane was delayed, and she was nervous about going home. The truth was, six years had passed, and the weariness that had once been her life, had chased her to LA. The guilt she carried for Ervin's death was still with her. The police never solved his case; the murderer remained free, and Reneata was left with no closure. And although she'd suppressed thoughts about her suicide attempt, it was becoming, more and more, the issue that haunted her dreams. *Why would I want to die?* she often thought. There was something more to her accident, but she wasn't sure what.

She was getting married. She was finally where she wanted to be. Cory loved her. Her feelings didn't make sense. Nonetheless, Dr. Brown was right, no matter how far she ran – whether she was in the Congo of Africa, sailing on the ocean, or lost in the bottom of an empty liquor bottle, she could not escape her past.

Stepping out of the yellow taxi, just before 6 p.m. on a Friday afternoon, the sun was bright, and the wind was still. Reneata stood in front of Gramps's old place, with her five suitcases tumbled over at her feet. After the taxi driver struggled to get her bags out of the trunk and off the backseat, the thin Asian man wearing red sneakers and black jogging pants, had asked if everything was good, before tucking the fifty-dollar bill she gave him into his pocket and driving away.

Gramps's old place was empty. No one had lived there for

years, after he married JoAnn's best friend and neighbor, Mill. He moved Mill and her four kids to a house in the next city. The only thing that remained in his old place was 30-year-old furniture and a porch swing he'd made for his new bride back in the 1950s.

The furniture was outdated and rickety, but it carried sentimental value. The front room was where Tess and Reneata would play house, and the back room had been built by Gramps to display Ervin's work. That's why Gramps refused to sell it. That house meant the world to him because it was the one thing he owned worth passing down to his grandkids.

The two-bedroom single-story home wasn't much to look at from the outside. It had a broken chain-link fence, a cracked cement driveway, and a cranky swing on the porch. But standing in front of the house, Reneata found herself gazing, thankfully, at the crepe myrtle tree just outside Gramps's bedroom window. Three birds perched in the tree chirped so loud it roused a feeling of homecoming and love, just what she'd been missing.

Struggling to get the five heavy suitcases up the steps and into the house, she made the last trip, quickly ate the hamburger and fries she had picked up while leaving the airport and jumped in the bed for a much-needed night's rest. Exhausted from the plane ride, she slept soundly throughout the night, without even a hint of a nightmare.

◆ ◆ ◆

Homecoming Day 2

"Not long now, baby girl," Ms. T said while planting a big red kiss just below the silk scarf tied around Reneata's hair. Reneata lowered her head and leaned in to meet her.

"You brought me some fudge bars, Ms. T?" Reneata whispered in her ear, trying to mask the unexpected quiver in her voice. A whiff of Ms. T's liquid foundation, peppermint, and White Diamond perfume made Reneata remember the magic of being back in the Deep South on a Sunday morning.

"I'll make you some," Ms. T said in the most beautiful Southern drawl Reneata had heard since crossing the Alabama state line some six years ago. "But you won't fit in that beautiful wedding dress if I do," she continued, and they both laughed before ending their warm embrace.

"I missed you, baby girl. Those Projects ain't been right since you...." Ms. T paused for a second before bating away tears. "You know what I mean -- you and my granddaughter, Gene, running around the neighborhood, playing jokes on everybody." She squeezed her eyelids together, as tightly as possible, but that didn't stop a stray tear from escaping. Reneata grabbed Ms. T's hand and held it until she could open her eyes again.

Ms. T's daughter, Gene's mother, Rachael, had died a year before, after battling addiction for close to twenty-five years. In and out of rehab and jail for most of her adult life, Rachael was a source of pain for Gene, and Ms. T, who loved her dearly.

"So, who gon' do your makeup?" she finally asked, after gathering her composure. Reneata released Ms. T's hand and returned to her stool in front of the mirror to finish applying a hint of pressed powder. She could see Ms. T's reflection as she removed two large bobby pins from the bright red chapeau cocked perfectly on the side of her head. As she lifted the hat in the air, she kicked off her red satin J. Renee pumps, and exhaled so loudly it startled Reneata.

"When the Bible taught about the 'full armor of God', do you imagine it was talking about this outfit?" she asked, almost to herself. Stumbling to the bed, she pulled her left leg over her right knee, and started massaging her foot.

"You alright?" Reneata asked, concerned and amused.

"War paint, heels, stockings, hats -- can't go to church without it," she said, ignoring Reneata's question altogether. "And pain, O'lawd, the pain, is the result. But you look good," she giggled.

Her tone, style, and laughter reassured Reneata that she was home. Nowhere on earth can a black woman look, smell, and taste so sweet and sanctified other than in the South. California was shaking off her quickly.

"So, who gon' do your make-up for the wedding?" Ms. T asked again, obviously jockeying for the job. For as long as Reneata could remember, Ms. T and Rachael loved make-up and fashion. And they had a gift for it. Women in the old neighborhood would line up at their doorstep to get their faces beat before heading out to church or the club. "Simple, honey. Keep it simple," Rachael would always say. "Nobody likes a clown outside the circus."

They taught Reneata and JoAnn everything they knew about clothes and make-up. Although Gene never cared much for either, she still admired her mother and grandmother, because no matter how broke they were, they made sure they looked like a million bucks. That's how all the women were in C-Way – black didn't crack and being broke didn't bury no good genes.

Ms. T hadn't changed much over the years. Her hair was short, gray, and curly, and her skin flawless, as if she'd bathed in milk and honey for most of her life. There were no regrets or shame lines on her face. No stray hairs or varicose veins. She was beautiful and shapely, full-figured in the world's eyes, but just as classy as the wealthy socialites Reneata had met back in LA.

"I don't know, maybe I'll do it myself," Reneata said, smearing on a little lip-gloss.

"You don't need much, Neta. Keep it simple."

"Rachael always said that," Reneata added, but this time the tears came racing to the surface of her own eyes.

Reneata felt puny in her silk robe and white bedroom slippers as Ms. T wrapped her large arms around her for the second time. Standing behind her chair while she faced the mirror, Ms. T said again, "So good to see you, Neta," and Reneata squeezed Ms. T's arms. A smile as big as a crescent moon appeared on her face.

"What you been up to Ms. T?" Reneata asked as she returned to her image in the mirror.

"Nothing much," she said, while walking back to the edge of Gramps's bed. She sat and continued to rub her tired, achy feet.

"Like that hat you were wearing," Reneata blurted. "Did you take home the best and biggest hat award at church today?"

Ms. T fell backward on the bed, laughing. "Don't make fun of our pastime, Ms. California," she said, pronouncing every syllable of the Golden State's name. "Church is eighty percent praising, ten percent flirting, and ten percent bragging. The South ain't changed, baby girl."

"You ain't changed either," Reneata said, now hearing the sweet return of her own southern drawl.

"How's that fiancé of yours, that I haven't met yet."

"He's a great guy, you'll like him."

"Tess told me his momma's in politics."

"Actually, state senator," Reneata said proudly.

"For California?"

Reneata nodded her head as she started to unroll her hair.

"How'd you like that? I mean, he has to be a big wig in California if his momma is in politics."

"He is," she assured her.

"You remember Deidra? Donnie Little's girl? She married a guy out of Atlanta who ran for mayor of some small town some years back and won. Now, every time she comes home she looks like she's traded ten pounds of body fat for twenty pounds of weave. Trying to stay relevant, I guess. Promise me you won't do that."

"No way," Reneata laughed. "Don't worry, Momma T, my head can't hold that much weave."

"Good," she snickered. "Now tell me about your fiancé."

"What you want to know?"

Ms. T wasn't only known for her J. Renee's and fancy hats. She was also the neighborhood gossip. Rumor was, she got wind that Tilley, a young mother from the old neighborhood, was pregnant with her fourth child the very night she conceived. Ms. T knew before the doctors could confirm it. Told everyone in the neighborhood that Tilley got pregnant by ugly Tyran's son, the night they had sex for the first time. Legend remains to this day that Ms. T had a 'special' connection to God that allowed her insight on the when and the whereabouts of everybody's business.

"So, you know? Did Gramps tell you?" Reneata blurted, while turning from the mirror to face Ms. T.

"Tell me what?" she asked, pretending to pluck lint from her red suit jacket.

"Don't play innocent, Ms. T. I know you. Plus, Gramps can't hold water ."

"Gramps ain't tell me nothing God didn't want him to share. What is there to be ashamed of? Details? Trust me, girl, everybody's details are messy, you ain't no different."

Turning back towards the mirror, Reneata caught an expression on Ms. T's face that made it clear that she knew more than Reneata wanted her to know. "Before Cory gets here, I want to set the record straight with you and Tess, but no one else. No one deserves to know about this or any other matter."

"Neta, don't be like that, don't get mad 'cause people care. And stop living like you don't need anybody, everybody needs somebody. Your sister cares about you, and while you were soaking up the sun in California, she sat in this old house and tried to fix the mess that you, your momma, and your brother left behind. So, don't ever let me hear you bad mouth her."

Reneata started to debate with Ms. T. She wanted to set her straight, but she was like family, and no matter how different they were, Ms. T was telling her the truth, and she needed to hear it. So, she nodded her head in agreement, then returned to the mirror.

"As I heard it, he cheated on you," she blurted.

"Yep." Reneata didn't look her way. Instead, she continued to pull the rollers from her hair until Ms. T got up to help.

"Your hair is beautiful," she said.

Reneata couldn't tell if she was trying to make her feel better or if she was sincere.

"Looking at you in the mirror makes me think about your momma. I don't think I ever told you this, but when me and JoAnn was in high school, she never really talked to me. I mean, we weren't friends or anything back then. Your grandfather owned this house and two cars. Everybody thought your folks had money. Crazy as it sounds, that was rich to us."

Reneata stopped untangling rollers and put her hands on her lap. She wanted Ms. T to do it for her. She wasn't pulling the rollers and tangled hair like Reneata was. Instead, she gently uncapped each one, slowly, as if it were the most important thing she would do all day.

When half the rollers were out of Reneata's hair, Ms. T continued to tell Reneata about JoAnn and their days together in high school.

"One day, Lester Evans asked me to a school dance," Ms. T said. "I think it was our junior prom, and I was too excited," she laughed, poking Reneata in the back, then smiling at her reflection in the mirror.

"Lester was special, I can tell," Reneata said, egging her on.

"Lester was the drum major. Six feet tall and lean. He could dance, I mean like someone you would see on TV, on *Soul Train,* or one of those music videos you kids like. I thought he was the most handsome boy in the school."

Ms. T. placed the rollers in the roller bag Reneata had made from an empty plastic grocery sack.

"Your mom liked Lester too; they had been messing around for a few months. That's why I was shocked when he asked me out." She paused for a few seconds, not to gauge Reneata's expression, but, instead, to relish the memory.

"You know I said yes, right?" Ms. T laughed, then nudged Reneata in the back again, this time with her knee.

"Bet you did, Ms. T," she cheered her on, tickled to see her smile so wide. "What did JoAnn say?"

"Lester picked me up for the dance in his father's old Buick. I remember the dress my grand momma made for me. It was lavender and white, with a pleated skirt and a spaghetti strapped top. It fitted me to a T. I was thinner back then, just a few pounds shy of that Beyoncé girl at her largest, which ain't much more than a twelve or fourteen. Curvy too."

Ms. T. stopped long enough to demonstrate, with the wave of her hand, her schoolgirl hourglass figure.

"He picked me up, didn't say a word. Just got me in the car and headed towards the school. When we got there, he reached over me and opened my door from the inside. Girl, I thought he was gon' kiss me, so I got ready. Puckered my lips up, closed my eyes, but nothing was delivered. When I opened my eyes, he was staring at me with a blank look. I remember thinking what he must have been thinking: 'What's wrong with this fool?'" she grinned, and poked Reneata again.

"Lester looked me square in the eyes and said, 'You cute,

Theresa, but not like JoAnn.' It felt like the wind had been let out of me. Halfway through the dance, he left me at the school while he made out with your momma in the car. He had obviously asked me to go to the dance because JoAnn had promised Terrence Oats he could be her date, and Lester wanted to make her jealous."

An awkward silence filled the room. Reneata didn't know what to say. She'd heard countless stories about how popular her momma had been in school. She knew about her reputation, but she had never felt like she needed to apologize for it.

"Don't look at me like that, Neta; this ain't no sad story, honey. I took it as a compliment. Someone thought I was pretty enough to rival the prettiest girl in school. Now, that felt good."

For an instant, Reneata didn't know whether to feel bad for Ms. T or to smile. She wondered if JoAnn ever knew.

"So, your fiancé cheated?" Ms. T picked up where she'd left off as if the Lester story connected their situations in some way.

"He really didn't cheat. He met someone at work during an event, and the woman saw an opportunity, and...."

"And he cheated?" Ms. T interjected without pause.

Rebelliously, Reneata pushed Ms. T's hands away and started pulling rollers again. Reneata's response had startled Ms. T., who took two steps back before dropping the rollers in her hand to the floor, then returning to the bed to sit down.

"What does it matter? I forgave him. He's a good man," Reneata said bitterly, staring at Ms. T's reflection in the mirror.

"No doubt," Ms. T said, clearly frustrated that Reneata wouldn't let her continue to help. "Guess you don't care to talk about it? Not because I'm nosy, but if I'd had a chance to tell my daughter, Racheal, something she needed to know, I would."

"Racheal knew better. She did just like Ervin. Got in them drugs and messed up. Plus, that has nothing to do with Cory and me. I mean, I'm sorry you lost her, and I feel for Gene, but Racheal had choices."

"What? What are you talking about, girl? Rachael didn't know nothin'!" Ms. T said angrily. "She was just like you... think you know everything, but you don't know nothin'! You ran out of here after Ervin died, like a million bees were on your tail. Never looked back to see what remained."

Reneata stood from the chair and turned in her direction. "Where is all this coming from, Ms.T? I've been here less than 48 hours and you already coming for me!"

"Just in case you want to run out of here again, I need to tell you something that your momma didn't have the guts to tell you. See, Neta, I've lived, loved, and lost. You young girls wouldn't know true love if it sat in your lap and tickled you silly."

"Okay, Ms. T. No disrespect, but I'm thirty-years-old, and not some little girl. If you came over here to give me advice, give it to me and then leave, so I can get ready for my wedding."

"Oh! Since it's like that, here's my advice: Good clothes can't cover a broken heart, and your fiancé cheating before you even get down the aisle ain't a good sign. But for you, it's not the worst thing you need to deal with right now. But it definitely needs to be dealt with."

Without prompting, Reneata's lips curled under and the whites of her eyes turned red. But she listened as Ms. T unleashed years of frustration. Reneata knew it was coming, but she wasn't sure how or when the message would be delivered.

She had chosen to leave; it wasn't the best decision for everyone involved, but for her, it had been the right thing to do. Ms. T was trying to save Reneata from something that she didn't think she needed to be saved from.

Cory did cheat, but only after his mother insisted he meet new girls before settling down. To his mother's disapproval, he'd moved Reneata into his home eight months after they met, and he had proposed five months later. In a way, Reneata understood her concern. His mother was trying to protect him. She didn't know anything about the girl who now consumed her son's life.

Cory apologized a million times. Brought Reneata ridiculous things she didn't need. Offered to go to counseling, but Reneata didn't want to go. She'd told him so many lies to cover up her past. So, when he cheated, she felt vindicated, for a while.

"Your barrels are filling up, baby girl," Ms. T continued. "Your momma would want me to tell you that. When we were your age, we had a family to take care of. There were no men around, other than the empty, broken ones in the neighborhood. When you knew love wasn't going to come easy, you stiffened your back and worked on what was most important - putting food on the table for your family. We worked our butts off to give our kids a decent life. We fought to preserve a sliver of ourselves, that's why we partied hard on Saturday nights and prayed harder on Sunday mornings. Nobody ever thought their future would be filled with food stamps, welfare checks, and ungrateful kids. You may not believe this, but we wanted big things, too. We wanted our 'California moment', but it didn't happen, and that's okay. We got what we needed in the end. But look at yourself in the mirror and ask, 'Are you getting what you need'?"

"Ms. T!" Reneata finally stopped her. "I'm happy; I got a good man, he loves me, and we are getting married. What happened to JoAnn is not my fault, and I've tried to be there for Tess. I'm sorry about what happened to Ervin. But it's my time, and I'm good. Everything is alright."

"I hear you, Neta. But, answer me one question: Why you came back to Alabama? You could have married anywhere, what brought you home after all these years?"

Reneata paused. "I don't know..." she finally admitted. "This is my home, why not come back?"

Ms. T huffed, then turned to walk away. Reneata watched quietly as she tugged to get her stockings back in place, then strapped on her J. Renee's. She didn't want to fight with that big red hat, so she tucked it under her arms, kissed Reneata on the top of the head, and headed for the door. But before walking across the threshold, she turned in Reneata's direction and said, "You didn't answer my question, but I'm gone leave it at that. Before your big day, you will have an answer for me, right?"

Reneata reluctantly shook her head in agreement.

CHAPTER 20: GRAMPS

"My baby's home!" Gramps shouted as Reneata ran into his arms. She refused to exhale until she cradled his big lumberjack shoulders.

"I've missed you so much," she cried, as he took a long, deep breath to meet her quivering embrace. The last time she'd seen him was in Atlanta, close to three years ago.

"Gramps, you're all round and fluffy," Reneata said while poking him with her index finger right above his bellybutton. "But I like it."

"Me too," he laughed. "Compliments of steroids, bad knees, and potato chips."

His wife, Mill, who was standing behind him, chimed in before he could say another word. "Sweet girl, please have no doubt I'm not trying to give him any more potato chips," she said, giving Reneata a bear hug and a kiss on the cheek.

"Mill. This is too surreal," Reneata said, almost to herself, as they embraced.

"I know, right?" she agreed. "Me and your old man?"

"Yes, but it's beautiful. How are the kids?"

"Gone. Out the house finally, and doing pretty well."

"That's great."

Over the next two hours, Reneata and Gramps talked about everything, from high school football championships to Tess's new job in New York. Gramps mentioned JoAnn only once, which left Reneata to believe they weren't on speaking terms. But she didn't want to pry. No. The truth was, she didn't want to know at all.

142

When Gramps excused himself to use the bathroom, Mill gently took Reneata's arm and led her to the kitchen. "Let's talk," she whispered, "he'll be gone for a while."

"Okay," Reneata responded hesitantly.

After pouring Reneata a glass of sweet tea, Mill started catching her up on what had happened over the years. As much as she didn't want to know, it was better coming from her. Mill and JoAnn had known each other for years. She was always like family. After her husband was killed in an accident at the steel plant, Mill took her four kids and moved into C-Way while the plant took its sweet time paying out his death benefits. A young mother, barely 25, with 4 kids and a great deal of debt. But from the looks of her and Gramps's two-story brick house and finely manicured lawn, she got what was due to her from the plant. In addition, she married a man who may have been almost twice her age, but who was a good man, who would never leave her side.

"JoAnn stopped speaking to me after she found out about me and Gramps's relationship. But in a way, I don't blame her. That ole man is old enough to be my dad," she laughed.

"As long as you're happy," Reneata said, while taking a sip of tea.

"I am."

"That's the only important thing. Plus, JoAnn was always jealous of any woman who took Gramps's attention from her, even me and Tess."

"Yea, she had a way about her, but I still, and always will, love her like a sister," Mill said. "She's doing the best she can right now. I mean, we don't see her much. Your granddad stopped going around so much after you left. He didn't like how she treated you kids. It took a toll on him."

"That's true for all of us," Reneata said, placing the glass on the table.

"I understand, but Neta, what do you want to know?" Mill leaned against the granite counter, waiting for what Reneata assumed was a conversation she longed to have.

Reneata had no idea that so many people felt she still owed them an explanation. Time and space had not resolved anything. It was as if Reneata had moved on, but everyone else was still waiting outside the hospital room doors for her to tell them what happened on the day Ervin died.

"What? What are you asking? Mill, I didn't come with a list or nothing. I just wanted to see my family and ..."

"Oh, I get it. You're not here to deal with all the things you refused to deal with in the past?"

"Something like that," Reneata smiled nervously. Mill was always a straight shooter, just like JoAnn.

"On the real, I just want to know if Gramps is okay."

"Yes and no," she said. "I mean, health-wise, he's okay, need to lose weight and get in front of a doctor more often. The rest is getting better."

"The rest?"

"Yes, Neta, the rest. There's a hole in that man's heart because of what happened."

"I can't fill it, Mill. That's why I left."

"The hell you can't," she said, sounding so much like JoAnn that Reneata had to do a double take. That southern-momma tenor got jabbed right at her, and she wasn't ready. "You helped make it, you can help fill it. Try, Neta, just try!"

"What do you want me to do? Time sure doesn't heal anything in real life. That only happens in fairy tales, I see," Reneata said, a bit sarcastically.

"Is that a question you think someone else can answer for you? The truth is time, God, honesty, and accountability will help you beat down them demons you are carrying. But never, just time alone."

"That's the truth. But what can I do now?"

"What can you do? I know, tell him you love him. Tell him you love yourself. Tell him the truth about your life. He raised every dime to send you on those trips. He wants you to enjoy your life, grow up, and see the world. Now, you are getting married. Are you good? Are you happy?"

"I don't know what to say, or whether it would matter," Reneata said.

"So, you came here with no plan … just to get married in a big fancy church wedding, then leave with the same hearts still broken and confused? You could have stayed in California for that."

"No. I mean. I plan to reconnect, to make amends."

"With who? JoAnn? See her. Tess? Pick up the phone. This isn't hard, girl. Reconnect. But start here. Do you understand? Start here!"

They sat in silence for a few minutes before Gramps came back into the room. When Mill saw him, she made up some excuse to leave them alone.

"I know what that's about," Gramps said when he heard her heavy footsteps on the hardwood stairwell.

"Mill is so lucky to have you. Honestly, we all are."

"That's good to know. I'm old now, not sure what good I am to her. She still young, still good looking."

"We all getting older," Reneata said, before grabbing his hand.

"I'm so happy to see you again, Reneata. I missed you,

baby-girl."

"Me too. But it was for the best."

"For who?" he asked.

"Everyone."

"I won't debate what was good for you, but for me, it was the worst thing you could have done. Leaving here the way you did."

"Gramps, none of it was easy. I had no choice."

"That's a cop-out, Reneata. I taught you better than that. Your life was tough. Bad things happened that we couldn't control, but we are family. You shouldn't have left the way you did."

"Nobody missed me but you, Gramps. JoAnn didn't care."

"Listen to me. Your mother loves you to the best of her ability, she helped me raise the money for your trips, and she asks about you all the time. When you have kids, you will understand."

"No, I won't. You loved me, Tess, and Ervin. She just tolerated us."

"You wrong. You know that? You have been wrong about a lot of things. Go see her."

"Why?" Reneata said angrily.

"Why? Because you think she hates you? She doesn't hate you. She's hurting, but it's not what you think."

Startled to hear him speak those words, Reneata sat in complete silence for a while, just staring at her glass. *JoAnn isn't angry with me,* she thought. She had no idea how much she had needed to hear that, until he said those words. Deep down, she had stayed away because she felt everyone hated her because of Byron, and all the misguided and immature things she did to make him happy. She wasn't sure if her actions led to Ervin's death, although they played a major role in how she saw herself.

"Reneata, you came home, finally, to deal with the truth. There's a lot for you to deal with, including JoAnn and Ty. Yes, Ty. That boy still loves you, and you never gave him closure. You'd been running for so long, even before Ervin died. In and out of the club, man after man. Your momma did the same thing."

"What do you mean?" Reneata said, ashamed to hear her grandfather speak truth to the matter.

"I will not ruin this chance for you to stop running and deal with your life. We are all happy you are getting married, but as my Rambler, this is the one trip I will not let you make without uncovering the truth. We are ready for you. Stop running and deal. See your momma and let her fill you in on what you're missing. Not me. It's not for me to do."

CHAPTER 21: BOBBY

Amorosa Avenue was lined with two-story, single-family homes, nice cars, and decorative mailboxes. Almost every house had a beautifully landscaped lawn and a cluster of rocking chairs on its front porch. The rental car was almost on empty, but Reneata took the scenic route anyway, cruising up and down Amorosa, taking in the southern charm and friendliness of every corner's bend.

She'd never visited this side of town when she was growing up. JoAnn rarely had a running car, so Reneata had been limited to city bus trips to the mall and a one-mile walk to school. It wasn't until after they returned from living with Brad that JoAnn became interested in how the other side lived.

Brad had a friend, Tramwick, who lived in the closest thing Reneata had seen to a mansion, right off the bay in Mobile. She, Tess, and JoAnn spent many Saturday afternoons there, playing in his pool and barbequing. Just being in his home and reveling in the finer things of life, Reneata had felt like royalty. Everything was clean and new. The bathroom smelled of lavender, and the dining room carried a hint of pine oil. The fruit was fresh, the yard was well manicured. She couldn't wait to take the hour-long ride to his place on those warm Saturday afternoons.

Tramwick had had a crush on JoAnn. It didn't take long before he went from inviting the entire family to his home to only inviting her. He always needed her help with some mysterious project that Tess and Reneata would be "too bored" to sit through. He would pick JoAnn up just before the day got started, and drop her off a little past three o'clock, so she would be at home to meet Brad at 4 p.m. sharp.

It wasn't long after Tramwick stopped inviting Tess and

Reneata to his house that Brad kicked them out. After arriving home early from work one day, he caught JoAnn and Tramwick kissing on his back porch. Reneata witnessed it all.

When Reneata stopped at 6677 Amorosa, she sat in the car for close to twenty minutes before opening the door. It took another five minutes for her to get the nerve to ring the doorbell.

A short Latino woman in a light blue blouse and pleated skirt opened the door just as Reneata was about to leave.

"May I help you?" she said in perfect English.

"Um," Reneata responded.

"Ma'am, can I help you?" she asked again.

Pulling herself together, Reneata gave her name and who she was there to see. Within seconds, the lady turned from Reneata, leaving the door slightly ajar, which allowed her time to admire the beautiful artwork that lined the main corridor of the house.

"Ms. Morris, you found me," Dr. Brown said, springing from a room beyond the foyer. Clad in a pair of linen shorts and a white polo, Dr. Brown's olive tan skin, buff physique, and tawny pompadour made him look more like a Malibu surfer than a shrink from a little town in Alabama.

"Found you? How did you know I was even looking for you?" she asked, a bit confused. But before he answered, Dr. Brown wrapped his arms around her so tightly she could barely catch her breath.

"Long overdue," he whispered in her ear, before releasing her from his embrace, then leading her through the door by the hand.

"Come in, Ms. Morris. How you been?"

"When did you get so southern, Dr. Brown?" she laughed.

"Call me Bobby. Can I call you, Reneata?"

"Of course."

A large wood-panel ceiling fan swirled rigorously as they took a seat on a tan leather sofa in the cozy family room just off the kitchen. On one side of the spacious room was the leather sofa, accented with peach throw pillows, and a round glass-top coffee table with mother of pearl trim. On the other side were two, large, cream-colored accent chairs, separated by matching mother of pearl trimmed end tables. Both tables held freshly cut flowers in crystal vases.

Dr. Brown stood behind one of the accent chairs – seemingly a bit too nervous to take a seat.

"Sorry for the cyclone, but it's close to ninety-five degrees today. I'm still not used to the southern heat."

"After all these years?" Reneata said, smiling.

"I'm still learning," he responded.

"Great seeing you," she said, staring undistractedly into his eyes.

Lowering his head like a bashful schoolboy, he blurted, "It's you," before playfully swatting the top of the chair with his hand.

"Yep. It's me," she said. "Six years later. In your home, no doubt. I mean, I'm sorry for just showing up."

"No need to apologize. I had a feeling you would come by."

"Why is that?"

"I got a call yesterday from the hospital. 'A pretty black girl' was looking for me," he snickered.

"And why did you think it was me?"

"Since I hadn't worked at the hospital in six years. I knew exactly who it was," he said, before walking from behind the chair to take a seat across from Reneata.

"You left? Why?" she asked.

"It had nothing to do with you."

"I hope not."

"I'm kidding, it had everything to do with you," he said, leaning forward with an even wider sugary smile. "Dishonored my oath to the profession my first time out the gate. I knew psychiatry wasn't for me."

"I don't understand."

"Yea, you do," he said confidently.

She gave him a slight smile, which he met with an easy nod of his head and a grin that confirmed that what she'd felt all those days while sitting in his office was true.

"What brought you looking for me?" he asked.

"I needed to say some things to you. I mean, I never got to tell you, 'thank you'."

"For what, doing my job?"

"No, Bobby Brown," she said, and they both laughed. "For going beyond your call of duty."

"I didn't do anything. I didn't do enough."

"Yea, you did," Reneata insisted.

Quiet for a second, Dr. Brown nodded his head and smiled, as if to say "thank you" without saying a word.

"What happened after I left?" Reneata asked, hoping to swat the uncomfortableness from the room.

"I stayed at the hospital for a few more months, then one day, I just resigned. The cute nurse walked into my office with a pan of warm honey buns and a cup of coffee, and I said, 'Thank you', walked out of my office, met my supervisor in the hallway, and told her that day would be my last."

"Damn. What brought that on? You were so young in your career."

"I couldn't help those people," he said.

"Those people?" Reneata asked, insulted.

"No. Not like that. I mean, I couldn't help the hospital. The staff. I couldn't meet the goals they set out for me. I couldn't give anything, hiding 'behind my books'. Remember?"

Reneata smirked, then nodded her head. She remembered the countless arguments they had had. She remembered the many lowbrow comments she'd made to one of the few people who had been trying to help her.

"Six years doesn't make you forget," he continued. "I was faking it. Just like you said. Thought my big degree would change who I was. Make me forget my sister and believe I had arrived. Instead of keeping up the charade, I got out."

"You ran," she said, feeling a bit of validity about her own actions.

"No. I evolved. You ran," he shot back.

"What? Me? No, I didn't..." but she stopped. He was right. No need to lie anymore. He was the one person who deserved the truth.

"I kept up with you, Reneata. I had no choice. You stayed on my mind for a long time." He sat back in his chair and watched as the ceiling fan blew a long curl of her hair in her face. After a few tries to tame it, she took a chunk of her bangs and tucked it behind her ear.

He watched her, the same way he had when she would spend hours in his office, reminiscing about her past and talking about the future.

"Why did you keep up with me?"

"Gramps and I got to be good friends."

This time, Reneata leaned forward, a bit confused. "What? Gramps? When did this happen?"

"He came to see me after you left for Atlanta, and we talked for hours. He is a great man, who loves you very much."

"He never said a word."

"There was no need to. I wasn't any good at the hospital, but I knew you. You are so much like me. I told him you would be back, because you wouldn't last long, living a lie."

"There you go, Dr. Brown, pretending to be psychic. You didn't know I would be back. Plus, why would Gramps believe you? You were part of why I stayed in the hospital for so long."

"No, you stayed because you needed to deal with your demons. And it's Bobby," he reminded her.

"You're right. I mean, not about the hospital. But we all have to deal at some point."

"So, you are here to deal with everything, now, right?" he asked, confidently crossing his legs.

"I guess so," she admitted, taking a deep breath.

"Why now?"

"I'm getting married."

"Really." A look of complete confusion came across his face before he dug deep to find a slither of congratulatory surprise. "Great for you," he continued.

"It is. He ... Cory Debose. My fiancé. He's a nice guy."

"Where are you living? Does he know?"

Slightly lowering her head towards the floor, she said, "We live in California. And he doesn't know."

"A relationship built on lies. Great start."

"I see you haven't changed," she responded, briskly.

"Reneata, you came to my house to talk to me. Not to your doctor, but to your friend. I told you I left the profession so I could *get real*. This is me being real."

"Is that what you do now, get real for a living?" she asked, trying to change the subject.

"Kind of. I'm what many call a 'life-coach'. I work with people who need direction; who can benefit from the truth without having to hear all the psychological mumbo-jumbo."

"Sounds like a low-paid shrink to me," she said, without thinking.

"It is," he replied confidently. "But it's so much more rewarding."

Saying that to Dr. Brown was ridiculous. Sitting in his half–a-million-dollar house, on his $3,000 leather sofa, while his maid brought her freshly squeezed lemonade and cookies. Who was she to insult him and his profession? It was time to go. She had overstayed her welcome, and besides, she wasn't ready for this. She stood to leave before further embarrassing herself.

"Sit here," he said, just as she reached for her purse. "Put that down on the table and sit next to me, I have something to show you."

Before she could make one move towards the door, he left the room.

Walking leisurely back into the room, seemingly unfazed by her opinion of him, he carried a book and a sealed eggshell colored linen envelope in his hand. Reneata was still standing in the same spot, with her purse under her arm.

"I have so much to do. I'm getting married here in a few days. I just wanted to let you know, and to invite you."

"Of course. Thank you. I mean, congratulations. I will try to make it."

"It would be great having you there," she said.

"Wait," he blurted. "Can you wait just a few more minutes?"

"Sure," she said reluctantly.

Bobby placed the envelope on the coffee table, then handed her the book.

"What is this?" she asked.

"It's for you. Read it."

"*The Magic of Woman* by Dr. Bobby O'Neal Brown."

"Open it," he said, flicking the ends of a red bookmark he'd placed a few pages from the front cover.

When she opened the book, there was a dedication that read: *To Ms. Reneata Morris: The beauty of being true to one's self is found in the honesty and grace of accepting what is bad and letting it inspire, compel, and empower a life filled with love. Your life - less ordinary - has moved me to be more than I could ever envision, in ways that you could never imagine. Thank you for your honesty.*

Reneata read the dedication several times before looking up to meet Bobby's smile. He knew she would one day find him. He had waited patiently, so that moment could be as special as it was. He was right; she needed to be there. She needed to know that her friend, the former psychiatrist, was good with what they shared.

"This is so amazing," she said, teary-eyed. "You didn't have to say a word about me."

"Yes, I did. You made me feel the pain I had tried to ignore about my sister's death. You made me know I wasn't alone. I only wish I could have done more for you. This doesn't fix that, but I wanted you to know that I see you as someone special."

"So, I was right, you are a low-paid shrink."

"Yea, and a bestselling author."

"Nice," she said, as she wrapped her arms around him. "This means more to me than you will ever know. You did well, I'm so happy for you."

When they ended their embrace, he gently took her face in his hands and asked her the question she didn't want to answer. Maybe because everyone – Ms. T, Gramps, and Mill – all wanted to know the same thing, but she didn't have an answer.

"Are you happy, Reneata?"

And there it was. Coming home meant facing the truth about something Reneata never, ever, thought about in the way others did. This idea of being happy was lost on her. She was comfortable, she was safe, she was taken care of ... but happy felt like a whimsical charade, like the Easter Bunny or Santa Claus. She didn't think about happiness; she just thought about what was real in the moment.

"Of course. I mean. Cory's a great guy," she said, sounding more and more like a broken record. Dr. Brown had asked if she was happy, and she tells him the state of another person's goodness, and not her own. Her life had moved from darkness – a place of sheer confusion, to night – a place where the stars could be recognized and admired from afar. Now, they wanted light, but she wasn't ready for that.

"No. That's not what I asked. Are you happy?" he repeated.

She slid her hands from his grip, took one step backward, and three deep breaths. It wasn't the question, which pierced her faux happiness like a butcher's knife gutting a fattened pig that made her sad. No. The problem she had was not the inquiry; it was the inquirer. At that moment, she realized how little her situation had changed. Six years ago, she had confided in Bobby about her past mistakes – telling him about Byron, the baby, the drugs, JoAnn - and now, as an adult woman who prided herself on being an overcomer, she realized that she was still standing at the starting line. She had gone nowhere, fast. Except for her travels, she was no closer to where she truly wanted, and even needed, to be.

"Are you asking me if I wrap my butchered wrist every night before bed with a warm towel, thinking if I could make the scars disappear, maybe the memory of that day would also vanish? Are you asking me if Cory makes it all better? Does he give me the kind of love that heals hurts and mends shattered glass?"

"Yes. That's what I'm asking," he responded.

Lowering her eyes toward the floor, she replied, "Maybe what you should be asking is, can Cory give me enough peace to get me through this life without wanting to cut deeper?"

Bobby took her hand again, just as he had while sitting in his small office in the county hospital. "Reneata, if what you are getting is not enough to help you forgive yourself and move forward, then it's not worth having. A slither of joy will never sustain you."

Again, pulling away, this time a bit angrily, Reneata stumbled, then fell against the accent chair before turning back in his direction. It was as if she were being chased by his judgment, his solid stare. He knew her. He knew the truth. She could not hide. But how could he judge her? What gave him the right to define her happiness?

"And you. Where's your good thing?" she chastened, looking around the room, as if this thing she inquired about was ready to appear out of thin air, like a magician's rabbit. "This big beautiful house. No wife, no children. Why?"

"I'm waiting patiently," he shot back. "Can you?"

He obviously hadn't heard her. Or he just didn't want to know the truth. "You don't know what I have," she reassured him. "It's good."

Bobby shook his head 'yes' when he clearly had no reason

to trust her at all.

"Wonderful," he said, arrogantly, after a brief pause. "Before you walk down that aisle, you tell this Cory guy the truth. Then you tell Gramps and Tess. Then you tell JoAnn how you feel, and you face your past, all of it. Do these things, and I will be the first smiling face you see when you turn to meet the world as Mrs. Reneata Dubose."

CHAPTER 22: TY

Journal Entry

My life is messy.

It had always been. I had been engulfed in a state of confusion since the day I was born. Fatherless, motherless in some ways, I'd trailed behind uncertainty, hoping to stumble upon the right path, but the right path was not for me. I was two people occupying one body. I was a young girl searching for completeness and a woman filled with anger and regrets.

"You miss me?" Cory asked, seconds after Reneata hit the answer button on her cell phone.

"Of course, I do," she said, standing over Gramps's gas stove, flipping three strips of bacon onto a cast-iron skillet.

"What you up to?" he asked. A question obviously prompted by the sizzle of the bacon.

"Pouring granola in my yogurt," she responded.

"Worried about fitting into your wedding dress?"

"You know me best," she replied, slathering a thick layer of mayo over a slice of freshly baked bread she'd picked up from Morrison's bakery that morning when she stopped in to say hello to her old co-workers.

"Don't get too skinny, Re. I like you thick."

"Don't worry, I'm keeping the curves, like them or not." When the grease from the bacon drained, she joined the mayo drenched bread with the three, thick, bacon strips, tomatoes, and lettuce. Then she sat at Gramps's rickety kitchen table and ate a sandwich she'd dreamed of for a while. Every time she had been seconds away from making one, she imagined her treadmill mocking her for her bad culinary choices.

"So, you miss me? You never answered," he continued.

"Of course, I do," she mumbled while chomping down the first big bite. "What are you doing?" she asked, repositioning the phone so she could get into the heart of the sandwich.

"You're not going to ask me if I miss you?"

And this time she had to giggle quietly into her napkin. Since she'd left California, Cory had been like a fifth-grader who liked a girl who didn't pay him any attention - pouty and overly concerned. She liked it...a little.

"I think you do. I mean, you've called me more times in the last seventy-two hours than in the last two weeks when I was in California. And the flowers were beautiful. The Tiffany earrings were nice, too."

"Only nice?" he shot back.

"Come on, Cory. I know you miss me, and it's our wedding, and everything, but don't spend another dime. Save it for the honeymoon. Where are we going, anyway?"

The awkward pause made his disappointment with her weak expression of excitement for the diamond earrings, apparent. He wanted her to be overwhelmed by his attention, but that wasn't the type of relationship they had. She sat at home, waiting for Cory and his mother to do whatever they do after work, after the gym, after the golf game, after church, or wherever they needed to be to network. Reneata was not a priority back in California. She knew he loved her, but this newfound puppy-dog love just wasn't their thing.

"It's a surprise," he said.

"Tell me," she insisted. When he began a prideful laugh,

she quickly put the phone on mute and took a big bite of her sandwich.

"Here's a hint. We are going to a place where the water is bluish-green, the people are caramel brown, have funny accents, and the land is rich in natural resources."

"No clue," she said, pretending she hadn't seen their first-class airline tickets from Atlanta to Rio de Janeiro.

"Trust me, you will love it."

Removing the phone from her ear, she caught the faded sound of someone knocking on the screen door.

"Hey, I need to go. Can I call you later?"

"Sure. Call after work. No. Call me after ten tonight, my time, mom has an event in LA she needs me to attend."

"Of course, she does," Reneata mumbled sarcastically.

"I didn't hear you, baby. What did you say?" he replied.

"I said, I love you."

"You too."

After placing the cell phone on the table, Reneata picked up her plate and walked to the front door. Standing with his back to her was a tall, muscular guy in denim jean shorts and a red t-shirt. He was slowly pacing back and forth.

"Hi, can I help you?" she said, talking to his backside.

"It's really you?" the stranger replied, as he turned in her direction.

"Ty! Oh my God," she said, and he gave her the most delicious smile she'd seen in ages. "Look at you." In a split second, she wiped her greasy hands on her sundress, ran her fingers through her hair, and smeared her lips with her index finger to fix the remaining lipstick she hadn't eaten off while devouring her sandwich.

"No, look at you!" He opened the screen door and took her into his arms.

He'd spun her twice before she begged him to stop. "Enough. Sit me down," she laughed.

"What are you doing here?" she asked, smitten by how handsome he looked.

"Didn't I make the list?"

"What list?" she said, smiling.

"Distance or years will never change you, girl. You made lists of everything when we were together. You would write down your club outfits. I remember you writing down everyone's birthday, every January first, and mapping out what present you would get them. You could make a list, but you refuse to stick to a plan."

"Funny. But unfortunately, you didn't make the list," she said, and he laughed.

"Why is that?"

"I was sure you wouldn't want to see me."

"You know me better than that."

"But, after everything that happened. How I treated you?"

"For another time," he stopped her. "I'm just happy to be here. Right now."

After giving her another hug, Ty walked to the couch and sat down.

"Are you okay?" he asked.

"I'm good," she said, standing on the opposite side of the coffee table from where he was sitting. "How did you know I was here? Never mind. Gramps. Right?"

"He's still the best guy I know. Love you to death. Just wanted to make sure we got to see each other."

The nervousness slowly subsided enough for her to take a seat in the chair next to the couch. Her legs went from a perfectly crossed x to a perfectly formed four, to just two well-manicured feet in open-toe sandals placed perpendicular to the floor. She was all over the place – nervous, anxious, and completely caught off guard.

"Yours?" he pointed to the sandwich on the table. "Bacon, mayo, and tomatoes?"

"Yea," she said, smiling.

"You haven't changed," he said, staring at her so intensely she didn't know how to react.

Ty still had enough sweetness in his eyes to make her want to crawl into his arms and never let him go. Nothing had changed about him. He was still the *beautiful lion* that she remembered. All the things she promised she wouldn't feel about him nagged her like a teething baby. No way could she still be this attracted to a man she had done everything to get away from. A man she didn't care enough about to let him console her during the worst time of her life.

"Yea, I have," she said, stepping back into reality. In fewer than six days, she would be walking down the aisle of the First Baptist Church of Tinsley to marry Cory. Not Ty. But Cory.

"Why would Gramps tell you I was here? I mean..."

"Because of the wedding?" he interrupted.

"Well, yes."

"I'm not here to stop your wedding, Neta, unless you want me to."

When she saw the grin on his face, she stood, picked up her sandwich, and started towards the kitchen.

"Did I say something wrong?" he asked, instantly regretting joking about the matter.

"Yes and no," she said with her back to him. "It's deep, our history, that is, and I didn't want to get into it, but I had a feeling I would see you."

"Look," he stopped her by gently touching her arm. "The past is the past. I just stopped by to say hello and wish you well on your wedding day. He's a lucky guy."

"I'm lucky, too. Things weren't that great before him. I mean… you understand, right?"

"I get it. He was there when you needed him most."

"Yes, he was."

Taking one step towards her before stopping, Ty shook his head in anguish.

"I'm not trying to rehash the past, Neta. But. I asked first. You said 'yes', then you disappeared."

"I thought we weren't going there."

"Right!" he blurted, as if what she said was enough to convince him that his feelings were wrong. "Anyway. Just a few days, and you'll be married." He mustered a slight smile.

"Yes, I will."

"Good luck, and it's great seeing you. You look as beautiful as I remember."

"You look great, too," she said, and in that very moment, it all came rushing back. Standing before her was the only man she'd ever wanted to be with for the rest of her life. He hadn't changed much since the days they spent lying under an oak tree in the park, kissing until their bodies felt like one. She'd seen his face a million times in her dreams, beckoning her to get better, wishing that she'd recover, get stronger, and come back to him. He should be her husband, but life had other plans.

Ty gave her a slight, shivering, smile, then asked for her forgiveness.

Confused, she stepped back towards the kitchen to put more space between them.

"What could you possibly need to apologize to me for?" she finally asked.

"I let you down. It took me years to realize that."

"You..." But then she stopped.

"I'm sorry, Neta. Please forgive me for what I said before. Forgive me for just showing up and pretending I hadn't thought of you every day. I'm sorry for not being there. Our plan was all I thought we needed to be happy. But I was a kid, running from my own issues. I just wanted you with me. I didn't look hard enough to see that you were trapped."

"I'm getting married," she said, accepting that it was the only thing keeping her from going too far. It was the reminder she needed that kissing his lips would ruin what she was so committed to building with Cory.

"I know," he responded.

"I love him."

"I understand."

"Do you?" she asked. "I've moved on."

"Yea, I know. But you didn't get a chance to know me ... the man that I became because of you."

"I didn't come back for you, Ty."

"I know," he said. "I'm not being selfish. I just want a chance for us to get to know each other again."

Reneata saw the sincerity in his eyes. She wanted that, too, but it was too late.

"Tell me, if you didn't come home to deal with the past, why did you come back? You had to know that everyone wants answers. You didn't leave behind people who didn't love you,

Neta. You left us all here, with so few answers, and we deserved better."

"I don't know. Maybe I returned to pay old debts ... clear my name," she said, now sitting on the arm of Gramps's old lounger.

"Who do you owe? That was six years ago, you made a mistake."

"You don't know what you're talking about," she interrupted.

"Yes, I do. You loved your brother, and he loved you. Life got overwhelming. Why wouldn't it? You had tried to hold down everything since the first day we met. Carrying your family, your torn relationship with your mother, your past, and her brother's addiction. It got the best of you. But don't you think it's time to let go of the past and move on?"

"Who could let this go!" she cried. "Who could let this madness go! I don't know if I am the reason Ervin was killed, but I do know I am to blame for trying to take my own life. It still haunts me."

Ty walked towards her, and she instinctively buried her head into his chest, as if there had been no distance between them.

"All these years, and you still hurting this deep," he said, stroking her hair. "What is this guy doing for you, if you still haven't grieved and forgiven yourself?"

She raised her head from his embrace and looked him directly in the eyes. "It's not Cory's fault. He doesn't know."

Feeling the rapid pace of Ty's heartbeat, she realized that he still loved her.

"You were never hidden," he said. "I see you. And if Mr. Wonderful doesn't, don't walk down that aisle."

She listened to his throbbing heartbeat for a few more seconds before reluctantly pulling away.

"I can't," she whispered.

Ty stroked her hair until her tears disappeared, then he left her with her thoughts, without speaking another word.

CHAPTER 23: TESS

Close to an hour passed, and Reneata was still sitting on the arm of the lounger, lost in her thoughts about Ty, when she heard another knock at the door.

"Who is it?" she said, wiping smeared eyeliner from beneath her eyes.

"Open the door," a raspy female voice demanded.

A smile crept across Reneata's face. "Still got those raggedy teddy bears and jacks ready?"

"What are you talking about, Re?"

Tess entered the house and gave her sister a big hug.

"You made it!" Reneata cheered, before kissing her on the check.

"Did I have a choice?" Tess grinned before nostalgically walking to Grandma Tess's picture, and smearing a two-finger kiss on her face.

"Gramps's old place," she said, tearing up.

"Yep. Good times," Reneata added.

"Look at you! My little sister, here in Tinsley with me."

Tess sported a nappy-afro that warranted a two-line part, and an afro pick stuck in the back of her head. Reneata had heard from Gramps that she was now gay, living with her partner in New York while she finished NYU. It was a heartache for a man who had grown up in the Baptist church, but he accepted it, even though Reneata never did. She believed Tess liked boys. She'd watched her sister make googly-eyes at too many dirty foot boys in the old neighborhood. If she was gay, it was the lifestyle she chose, and not one she had been born into.

"So, this is the new you. I see."

"You like," Tess said, sounding like a hoarse, fourteen-year-old boy.

"Not really, but I heard you were trying to give Gramps a heart attack."

"Everybody can't be a black Barbie-doll like you, Neta."

"You right about that, too much work, combing hair and putting on a dress. Why not just cut off some dude's jeans and steal a t-shirt from the Goodwill?"

"It's my thang," she smiled.

"You still my sister, right?" Reneata said jokingly.

"For now," Tess shot back.

"Well, that's good enough for me. As long as you can straighten your hair and put your hips in a dress for the wedding."

"For you, yes, but only if you give me the same respect when it's my turn."

"You getting married?" Reneata said sarcastically, as Tess covered her mouth to laugh.

"No, but maybe one day," she responded.

"Boy, Girl, Boy/Girl?" Reneata grinned.

"Let me surprise you," Tess said, and they both laughed.

They gave each other another hug, then sat at the kitchen table to talk.

Three hours passed, and the sisters were still giggling like little girls catching butterflies in the tall grass. It felt like something they'd never experienced before. It felt like a sisterhood.

They'd never had that. Reneata spent her childhood trying to be the mother Tess needed, but she'd missed out on the chance to be her sister and friend.

The rain finally stopped, after forty-five minutes of a heavy downpour. Sitting in her rental car, listening to an old R. Kelly CD, Reneata watched the door of JoAnn's house, hoping that no one was home. The gravel driveway was littered with crumpled newspapers that blew in from trash cans as far as a block away. The plants on the porch had browned, and her swing, the one Ty and Reneata would sit in for hours, talking, was hanging from a half-broken chain.

This was where it all happened – a place with a past as dark as a sunless sky. Nothing much had changed, including the cracked cement right where the porch steps began, the very one that tore open Reneata's bare feet as she ran into the house six years ago.

For years, Reneata wondered what her life would've been like if her phone had never rung. Or better yet, if she'd never met Byron and his brothers.

JoAnn saw her. She was sure of it. Walking in and out of the house in her raggedy, floral-printed house dress, she pretended to care about the lifeless plants on her stoop. She tried not to stare. Keeping her head down, and one hand in her pocket, like she had something to hide.

Reneata could tell she was fully dressed underneath her housedress. Strange. It was as if she were preparing to run if things didn't go the way she wanted them to.

Convinced it wasn't the way she wanted this meeting to happen, Reneata started the car and slowly drove away. Maybe another day. Maybe never.

CHAPTER 24: THE TRUTH

"Look at you," Bobby said when Reneata approached the small café table at Nydia's Coffee House. The bustling upscale Bistro was filled with businesspeople chatting with colleagues and talking on their cellphones. Bobby sat at a table that was semi-secluded and separated from the rest of the patrons. It was near a window, on the side of a small bar surrounded by three bar stools.

Reneata was the only black woman in the room, which wasn't a big deal to most of the patrons, with the exception of a group of gay guys sitting in the corner, who appeared disappointed to see her join the handsome and well-clad Dr. Brown.

The grin he gave her was contagious, and putting aside her uneasiness from seeing JoAnn, she returned to him the brightest smile she could muster.

She'd done that a lot lately. Smile, that is. Even after the pain of seeing Ty, she found it in herself to pull it together without getting down or picking up a bottle of wine.

All dressed up, Reneata hadn't spared one moment in the mirror that morning. She had a busy day ahead. Three back-to-back meetings with the pastor, caterer, and florist, and a friendly coffee date with the one person she feared the most, but who happened to know her best.

"I was shocked to hear from you," Bobby said as she sat down at the table.

"I promised you an invitation, so I came to deliver." She handed him a gold-sealed envelope made of pink parchment paper.

"I forgot," he admitted, in a tone that seemed a bit deflated, and not like the one he'd welcomed her with.

"You forgot my wedding?"

"You did mention something about getting married. I just thought."

"What?"

"Never mind," he said, turning to watch as the couple near them stood to leave.

"You thought I wanted something else?"

"Not at all. There never has to be a reason to meet with a friend," he smiled.

"Okay, then," she said.

"Well. If nothing else, this makes us friends," he concluded, holding up the invitation as if he were auctioning it off to the highest bidder.

Before turning to order her coffee from a blond-haired young girl with a silver lip ring, she caught an awkward glance from Bobby that she hadn't expected.

"You were my shrink. Nothing changes that," she said, handing the waitress the menu. The awkwardness was proof they had unresolved issues that had festered since their last visit.

"So, it's wrong that I know things about you, or just being here is wrong?"

"Both. Neither. I mean, it doesn't matter," Reneata said.

"It matters to me if it matters to you," he said.

Reneata smiled, recognizing, that despite everything, he still wanted to see her happy.

"There she is," he announced to the rest of the patrons, with a silly grin that made them both laugh.

An hour and three cups of coffee later, they were still talking. The room was partially empty, and the waitresses were preparing for the lunch crowd.

"Is that the real reason you left the hospital, to get away from crazy-Katie?" Reneata asked, referring to the blonde nurse at the hospital who Bobby admitted dating for a while.

"You would think," he said, "but no, as I said before, it was you."

The waitress walked to the table with a pot of hot coffee. Covering the top of her empty cup with her hand, Reneata caught her eye, and she got the message.

"Me?" she said, as Bobby watched confusingly as the waitress turned around without filling his cup. "I don't understand."

He gave her an unsettled look.

"Something wrong?" he asked.

"Yea. I mean, what had I done to make you leave your job?"

"Did you read the book?"

"No. Should I?"

"Yes. That's why I gave it to you. You inspired it."

"My case? My situation with Ervin?" she asked.

"Yes, and no. I mean, you. You inspired it. Your situation with JoAnn. Your love for your family. And what happened to you."

"You gave details?" she asked, struggling to stay calm. She had read the dedication a few times but was saving the book for her flight back to California.

"No. I didn't give details or mention your name. It's fiction. It's a look into your condition."

"My condition? What condition? Sadness over my

brother's death? What else is there?"

"You don't remember?" he asked, confused.

"Do you think I would be asking if I did?"

"How are you sleeping, Reneata?"

Confused, she looked around the room. "What does that have to do with anything?"

"Just tell me. Humor me."

"I don't," she admitted, lowering her eyes to the floor.

"You don't sleep?"

"Well, sometimes. But that's not odd. I have a lot on my mind."

"Ok. What do you dream about when you sleep?"

"This is silly. I dream about nothing. Why?"

"Do you remember that night? Do you remember what happened?"

"Of course, I do."

"Not Ervin. But what happened at the club a few nights before."

Frustrated that he was trying to rehash the past, she struggled with what to say next. He knew her story, all that she remembered, anyway. Why take that moment to try and make her reveal more?

"Doc, either tell me where this is going or stop asking these questions. I'm not on your couch, anymore."

"Of course not. You don't have to answer. Let's talk about something else."

"No. You're trying to tell me something, and I need to know."

Bobby became unusually quiet. Reneata didn't say a word. He'd been trying to tell her something since before she left the hospital, but they never got around to it. It was time to clear the air.

"Something's been missing?" he finally asked.

"Truthfully? Yes. But I don't know what. I don't sleep. I haven't slept without taking a sleeping pill in six years, until the night I arrived back in Tinsley. But that can't be odd, considering what I went through."

"Anything else?" Bobby asked. "Tell me."

"Yes. I've had some bad days."

"What does that mean?"

"I've visited a few doctors over the years. Got my tune-up and went on."

"Tune-up?" he asked. "Medicine? Counseling? What does that mean?"

"Yes. That," she admitted, almost in a whisper. "I went, maybe, four times. I wasn't feeling well. Things weren't right. I even went to see a minister, once. I was drinking at the club, passed out somewhere, and found myself stumbling into a church."

"What happened?" he asked.

"The pastor took me into his office and let me sleep it off. He later gave me a few bible verses and invited me to the next Sunday service."

Pastor Warren had been alone, praying in the pew when Reneata, who was high and lost, entered the church early one Sunday morning before daybreak. He took her in, wrapped his suit jacket around her shivering body, and let her sleep in his office, undisturbed for hours. When she woke, he handed her a decent dress to put on, to avoid the judging eyes of his congregation, and a Bible with five bookmarks already placed where the bible verses were that he wanted her to read. He hugged her tightly before she left and told her his doors were always open. No judgment. No questions. She doesn't remember him asking her name. She had never told anyone until now. She had never wanted to admit that things had gotten so bad. But this happened just before her first trip abroad. When she got the money and the airline ticket from Gramps, she took it as a sign that the pastor's prayers had worked.

"I never wanted you to leave the hospital," Bobby said. "You weren't ready. Your grandfather can be very persuasive, but he didn't understand that you were nowhere near being healed, or even placed on the right track to survive the attack."

"The attack? On Ervin?"

"No. On you," he blurted. "I thought, one day, you would remember, but listening to you now makes it clear that your condition is possibly irreversible. The truth, Reneata? I didn't want to be the one to tell you, but you were raped."

"No. I wasn't. That's ridiculous. Are you still talking about losing my virginity to Byron at twelve? That's not rape, that's a bad decision," she said, trying to force a smile.

"No," he grabbed her hand. "You were raped in the restroom of Savoy's nightclub, two days before you tried to commit suicide."

"What? What the hell are you talking about? That never happened!" Reneata said while doing everything she could to keep from exploding. They were in a public place, not the ideal location to have this conversation. "Is this a joke? Are you angry that I went on with my life without your help? What are you saying?"

The squeal of her voice and her abrupt jolt from the chair caught the attention of the remaining three coffeehouse patrons.

"Reneata, calm down. Please. Take a seat," Bobby asked politely.

She hesitated, then slowly returned to her seat.

"Hear me out, two days before you were admitted to the hospital, I was on duty in the emergency room at Thomas-Elm Hospital when a call came in about a young woman who was found unconscious in the lady's restroom at a nightclub on Elm Street in Tinsley. She was intoxicated and had passed out. When she was found, her clothes were torn and bloody, and it appeared that she had been sexually assaulted."

"Elm Street? That's where Savoy's is," she recalled.

"Do you remember anything?"

"No. I mean, I know the place, but I never heard about no rape case."

"It was very late when they found her. The club was practically closed. The restroom door had been locked from the inside or jammed shut, so no one found her until the cleaning crew got there."

"What does this have to do with me?"

"It was you, Reneata."

"No, it wasn't. Don't you think I would remember that? Don't you think I would know that I was raped? What are you talking about?" She stood, again, to leave. But this time, Bobby watched in silence as she tossed a fifty-dollar bill on the table for the waitress, gathered her purse, then headed out the door.

Reneata was convinced that Bobby was trying to hurt her. There was no other explanation. It was a mistake to go there, to come home.

In haste, she stumbled on a cracked sidewalk trying to get her keys out of her purse while walking to the car. Landing on her knees just steps away from the car door in the parking lot, she began to cry. She had no recollection of being raped, but she knew, deep down, that wanting to hurt herself had something to do with more than the death of her brother.

Bobby walked up behind her, gently grabbed her arm, and helped her to her feet.

"Don't go like this, Reneata. I'm just trying to help you."

"Help me? This is not how you help me!"

"You have what we call post-traumatic stress syndrome, coupled with acute memory loss. The longest case I've ever seen," he said. "When you showed up at my house, I thought you knew. I thought you had remembered. But after six years, you are still suppressing everything."

"These are lies. Ugly lies! I'm not sure what you're getting out of it, but I can't stay here and listen to this." Reneata's knees were bloody and aching from the fall.

"Wait," he insisted. "You need to hear this."

For as much as she wanted to believe that he didn't care about her happiness, she remembered how kind he was to her when she was in the hospital. So, she turned around and let him finish.

Holding her trembling hands in the parking lot of the coffeehouse, Bobby asked, "Are you ready?" She took a deep breath, then shook her head, yes.

"Who knew besides you?" she asked.

"Everyone."

"Gramps?"

"Yes. He made the hospital staff promise not to push you to talk until you were ready. You were going through so much with your brother's death. You were hallucinating and demonstrating a fantasy-prone personality. Realizing the rape, your grandfather thought, would drive you to hurt yourself again. The doctors were against it. I was against it. But when you never brought it up, and your health began to improve, we knew that it was only a matter of time before Gramps would get you out."

"I want to believe you, but a few sleepless nights don't add up to what you are accusing me of."

"What do you dream about?"

"Nothing. I mean, I dream about Ervin. Who wouldn't, in my situation?"

"Ervin was the person you called after you came to. He came to the club. He tried to get you to see the doctor, but you wouldn't go."

"How do you know all this about this rape victim?"

"I got the call. I was on-duty at the hospital when it happened. They gave me a description of you, your name, and asked me to come down to the club. But that's not standard protocol. I couldn't leave the hospital, they needed to bring you to me, and it had to be your decision."

"No! No way. This is ridiculous. I don't know why I'm still here listening to this."

"You came home to find the truth. Running away didn't rescue you. The sleepless nights, the dreams, the weariness. You knew something was missing."

"I missed my family. That's the weariness. That's all."

"Okay, Reneata. I won't push this. I told your grandfather I would tell you. And I have."

"My grandfather? What does he have to do with this?"

"After you left. We talked often. He came to see me. He told me about your mom, the things she's gone through. He told me more about your relationship with Byron and Ty."

"My mother? What could he tell you about her? How she never came to see me at the hospital? How, in six years, we've spoken less than five times?"

"He told me why she struggles. You need to see her, too. You need to deal with that relationship."

"Let me get this straight. I was raped in a dirty bathroom at the club. Two days later, my brother is murdered, possibly by my old boyfriend in my mother's house. After his murder, I attempt to commit suicide, but I don't know exactly why. And now you are telling me that I have suppressed the memory of the rape, which is possibly the real cause of my suicide attempt? None of this makes sense to me. I'm sorry."

"No one really knows the truth about what happened to your brother, but we believe it had something to do with your rape. He was high when he was shot to death, but he had tried to get clean. The night at the club, he lost it. His baby-sister had been raped, and he couldn't do a thing. He went looking for the guys who hurt you. He never found them. It's possible that he may have pissed off the wrong people, either trying to buy drugs or trying to take revenge for what happened to you."

"You brought me to a coffee house to hear this crazy story?"

"You invited me, remember?" Bobby said.

"Regardless! This is insane. I'm getting married.

Maybe that's why you are telling me this. Maybe you thought there was something more between us. Maybe you want me to depend on you?"

"If I wanted to disrupt your life, I would have looked for you after you left the hospital. You weren't ready to leave. You were very sick, but your grandfather didn't want you there anymore. He made me promise never to bring up the rape unless you brought it up first. You never did."

"You are talking about my grandfather like he was the hospital's administrator. That wasn't his call."

"No. But we had no reason to keep you so long. I fought for more time to try to get you to talk, but my time ran out."

"I'm not sick anymore. Look at me. I'm happy. I'm getting married."

"You deserve to have all the pieces to the puzzle. I hope you understand."

"No. I don't understand! I mean. I knew something was missing, but that's expected. I ruined my relationship with Ty. I hurt Ervin. I disappointed Gramps and my little sister. Byron would never have been a part of our lives if it wasn't for me; Brad either. I made so many mistakes."

"Stop! You were hurt. You have been hurting since the day you found out about Ervin. Twelve years old, wondering if someone you loved would die. First, you dreaded that your worst nightmare would come true – Ervin would OD, your mom would go shortly after from heartbreak, and you and Tess would be left to navigate this world alone. You were, like me, filled with guilt and shame. Ervin was the addict, but so were you. He was addicted to heroin, and you, even to this day, are addicted to guilt and pain."

"That's not true," she insisted.

"You felt guilty about what happened between you and Byron. You felt guilty for what happened between your mom and Brad. You felt guilty for loving Ty and wanting to leave your family in Alabama and start over. Then you felt guilty for letting him go."

"You think I'm still fighting the darkness?"

"Are you?" he asked.

Reneata paused, took a deep breath, and tried to come up with an answer to satisfy them both. But there was no false reasoning that she could give.

"The truth? Yes. I've fought it every day since I left, and even before," she admitted.

"Reneata, you are not where you come from. You are who God made you to be. Let go of all the guilt, and I promise, you will find your way out of the darkness."

He grabbed her tightly and tucked her head into his chest. "I left the profession because it conflicted with my true beliefs. I believe that we all live two parallel lives – one consumed by light, and the other, by darkness. God lives in the light, and He and only He can help us defeat the darkness. We can give our struggle different scientific names, prescribe medication, and see the finest therapists to combat it. We can even believe it's about our past - you taught me this, you know. But the reality is, our fight must be to remain in the light. We must keep the light on within us, and no matter how dark our world may get, we must never give in to it. Never."

She slowly pulled her weary body from his arms, grabbed her purse from off the ground, and then drove away.

CHAPTER 25: UNCLE TOOT

"You got out this time," JoAnn said, as Reneata entered her house.

JoAnn looked like she hadn't aged one day since Reneata left. Still beautiful, but undoubtedly sad, in a way only a mother who'd lost her child could understand. Her hair was curly and flowing down her back, and her face was covered with just enough lipstick and foundation to convince her daughter she was waiting for a man to stop by.

"You look good," JoAnn said, puffing on a half-smoked cigarette.

Placing her purse on the counter, Reneata walked to the dining room table and took a seat across from JoAnn.

"You look good too," she responded, after a few minutes of staring at all the familiar relics of her past life. Her life had changed, the last time she entered JoAnn's house.

Nonchalantly picking a stray flake of tobacco from her tongue with her index finger, JoAnn said, "So, you're getting married, I hear."

"Yes."

"No invitation for your momma?"

Fumbling with her chandelier earrings, Reneata fought back the rising anxiety in her head. "Didn't think you would come," she replied, after a few minutes of thinking long and hard about how she wanted to answer the question.

"Why is that? Don't think the church can handle my kind of evil?" she laughed.

"Something like that," Reneata said, under her breath.

"I heard God forgives fools and babies. Don't you think I qualify?" She smashed her cigarette in the ashtray, then slowly blew out a cloud of white smoke.

"I wouldn't call you a fool. Definitely wouldn't call you a baby."

"That's nice of you."

"I came by to see how you are doing," Reneata said, as kindly as she could muster.

"Different day, same bullshit," JoAnn snickered.

Wiping her hand on the wooden kitchen table, Reneata said, "This place looks the same. I see you haven't dusted since I left six years ago."

"Who I got to dust for? You haven't been here. Tess comes home once a year. Gramps and Mill over in that good neighborhood ... they aren't coming this way. The rats and roaches find the dust enchanting. So, I'm good."

"Still bitter, I see," Reneata scolded.

"I ain't bitter about nothing," JoAnn replied as she rolled her eyes. "My oldest daughter can't invite me to her wedding, and still won't talk to me, and all."

"Well, if you wanted to talk, you knew where I was. You sent me things – I'm grateful for them, but we just never have much to say to each other."

"Last I heard, you went from Georgia to California. What number did I have?"

"That's your excuse; you didn't have my phone number? Well here." Reneata walked to her purse, pulled out a business card, and slid it across the table to JoAnn before returning to her seat. "That's settled."

"Fancy," JoAnn chided, before kissing the back of the card, leaving a lipstick print on the glossy paper. "Little Reneata from the hood has arisen. Proud of you with a business card and all."

JoAnn rolled her eyes, then shoved the business card into her blouse pocket.

"This was a mistake. I shouldn't be here." Reneata rose to leave.

"Wait. Where are you going?" JoAnn sharply asked.

"I thought we could talk like civilized adults, but that can't happen."

"Girl, please! Talk about what?"

"Ervin!" Reneata shouted.

Shaking her head, JoAnn rolled her eyes towards the ceiling, then attempted to get Reneata to sit with a flick of her wrist. But she refused to take a seat.

"Sit down, girl!" she finally demanded. Hesitantly, Reneata returned to the table and took a seat.

"What about Ervin you want to talk about?" she asked, after tapping both ends of a new cigarette on the table.

"What happened?"

"Why bring up this stuff? He was sick. Sick!" she shouted. "Twelve years of watching that boy kill himself. It was bound to happen, just as it did."

"But what happened, exactly? Did something happen to me at the club?"

"The club? What club? Are you talking about Savoy's place? What do you want to know about that for? Bad times, girl. Leave it alone."

"What about you? What happened to you?"

"Me. Nothing happened to me. I mean. I did my best with y'all kids. But that's every momma's story."

"Stop the bullshit," Reneata yelled. "Stop running, and just talk. Stop trying to act like you aren't as torn up on the inside as I am. This is our one time. I need to know what happened! I need to put this to bed!"

JoAnn stared at the glass ashtray before spinning it with her index finger. Her eyes intentionally diverted from Reneata's. It took Reneata a few seconds to realize that she was holding back tears.

"Look at you," JoAnn finally said, still staring at the ashtray.

"Look at me!" Reneata demanded, and JoAnn slowly raised her eyes to meet her daughter's painstaking stare.

"You just like me, but one hundred times better," she said, and the tears started to flow. "All I wanted was a good life, although I didn't always know what that meant. For the longest, I thought your daddy, or Tess's daddy, or some man would give it to me. I have the best daddy of all, but he's old school. Old-school values. He knows how to treat a lady. I looked for that, but no one has them skills no more."

"Gramps is a good man," Reneata nodded, struggling to hear her mother without judgment. "It set the bar high for all of us. I've tried to find someone like him for myself. It's not easy."

Wiping tears from her face with the back of her hand, JoAnn continued, "Yea, but you had that with that boy, Ty. I can't lie, that's when I started hating myself the most."

"What?" Reneata replied.

"You found what I wanted - a good man. It hurt like hell to see you get him."

"Wait?" Reneata stopped. There was no way JoAnn could be saying what Reneata thought she heard. Reneata stiffened her back and raised her body towards the edge of the table. "You telling me you were jealous of Ty and me?"

"I wouldn't say jealous, Reneata. I just saw how happy he made you."

Growing angrier by the second, Reneata continued, "Isn't that what every mother wants for her daughter, happiness? You do understand that I am not you, JoAnn!"

"Call me momma or leave!" she yelled, slamming the ashtray to the table.

"You never acted like my momma. Think about what you said, you don't want me happy."

The very idea brought them both to tears. JoAnn was being honest, but it was difficult for Reneata to accept. They were more different than she once believed. Every man that abandoned JoAnn, and each child she bore without a father, made her dreams seem less obtainable. She'd made her mistakes, she carried her guilt, but Reneata was pushing hard to make sure her fate was not the same as her mother's. Ty represented that. His love for her, his fortitude to stay was a reminder of all JoAnn had lost.

"You hated Ty. You wouldn't even let him in the house when he came to see me. You accused him of cheating on me because he was friendly with the girls at the bakery. I believed you."

"Ty was not Byron," she said, in a tone that sounded like an apology. "That piece of nothing, no good drug dealer you loved so much."

They had never spoken much about Byron, after returning from Brad's, but Reneata knew JoAnn resented her for her role in forcing the family to leave Tinsley. "I was young, impressionable. I made a mistake."

"A mistake? You screwed the dope-man who supplied that junk to your brother. We had to run away from everything because of that boy. I lost everything because of Byron!"

"And you still mad about it?" Reneata said, disgusted. "All

this silence. All this hatred because of Byron? He didn't make Ervin use, nor did I. The only person at this table guilty of that is you!"

"Me!"

Tears streamed from JoAnn's eyes in a way Reneata had never seen before.

"What did I do?" JoAnn screamed. "I wasn't perfect, but I wasn't sleeping with his supplier either."

"That's all you remember? Not the isolation? Not the lack of love? Just what I did? Don't forget … you slept with him, too!"

"To help Ervin. To save you. Don't you get it?"

"No! I don't." Reneata jolted from her chair. "I never understood much about you. You were a horrible mother. Every man that walked into your life got more from you than any of your kids could. You are the reason Ervin got high! He got high to survive another day in this cold house with you."

"Get out! Get the hell out of my house!" JoAnn screamed, as Reneata hastily snatched her purse from the counter. "Go marry the fool that cheated on you. You deserve everything that happened to you. At Savoy's, and here. You did nothing to help your poor dying brother."

"What did you say?" Reneata asked, after turning and walking towards JoAnn.

"You heard me." She didn't flinch.

"No, what did you say about Savoy's? What does Savoy's have to do with anything? Don't tell me something really happened! Please don't tell me that," she cried.

When it dawned on JoAnn that Reneata had no idea what she was talking about, she calmed down and asked her to take a seat.

"No! Just tell me!"

"It was a long time ago. No reason to hash up the past."

"Momma, I need to know. Dr. Brown said I was hurt at the club a few nights before Ervin died. Is that true?"

"Don't you remember?" JoAnn asked, pushing back from the table, then walking to the kitchen. Reneata could hear her opening the refrigerator, then pouring a beverage into a glass. She stood in the same spot, with her purse tucked tightly under her arm.

"I don't remember anything," she finally said.

"I tried not to remember too," JoAnn said lethargically. "You know. When it happened to me. I tried not to remember."

"What are you talking about? What do you mean – when it happened to you?" Reneata asked.

"Uncle Toot raped me when I was a little girl. Barely eight," JoAnn said. Her voice quivered so hard that her words didn't seem to be hers at all.

"Uncle Toot?" Reneata muddled.

"He was drunk," she continued. "Gramps left me at his house to help clean up for the week. Toot started at me in the bathroom. Raped me. Beat me up bad."

"Wait," Reneata said. "I don't understand."

Uncle Toot died when Reneata was nine-years-old. The first time she saw him was at his funeral. She'd had no idea Gramps had any living family, until that day. She remembered a big black man with salt and pepper hair lying in a casket, who looked so much like Gramps that she began to cry. JoAnn sat in the pew and watched as Ervin and Reneata bid the great uncle they had never known, goodbye.

Uncle Toot didn't talk much. He wasn't educated, but he

could sing. One Sunday each month, JoAnn and Gramps would drive twenty minutes north of Birmingham to hear him sing at a small storefront church.

He didn't have much. He barely worked a steady job, but he was good with his hands, and he made enough money doing handyman work for the people in the small town where he lived to keep his mobile home in the sticks going.

Uncle Toot had never married or had kids. His life was filled with work and church and the occasional visit from Gramps and JoAnn on Sunday afternoons.

Gramps and Uncle Toot would sit on his front porch, smoking tobacco, drinking whiskey, and reminiscing about their childhood in Florida. Uncle Toot would always get drunk and pass out. Once he was sound asleep, JoAnn would clean the house while Gramps went to the corner store to stock the refrigerator with food for the next few weeks. It was his way of taking care of his little brother.

One Sunday, just as Gramps drove off down the red dirt road, Uncle Toot awoke from his drunken stupor, after passing out on the porch. Dragging his big body from the rocking chair on his tiny porch, he stumbled inside, and into the bathroom, where JoAnn was wiping down the sink. Startled, she turned to say something, but he was half-awake and half in a daze. He pushed past her and started urinating in the toilet as if she weren't there. Crammed against the wall behind him, JoAnn reached for the door, but he was too large to pass.

When he reached for the doorknob, they made contact. But he was her uncle, drunk and unaware. She wasn't afraid, instead, she thought the encounter would be something they would laugh about when she got older. So, she breathed lightly and waited for him to leave the room.

Just as she thought he was prepared to exit, the lights went out, and before she could call his name, to wake him from his daze, he had forced his body against hers and touched her in a way she didn't understand.

"When it was done, my life changed," JoAnn said. "I lay in splattered blood, and my uncle, the only family I had, except my father, sat on the front porch and cried. I'd never heard a man cry like that before."

"I eventually passed out from the pain. When I came to, Gramps was driving me to the hospital. He was crying. Sick with anguish and covered in blood. But not mine. Gramps beat Uncle Toot to one inch of his life. Told the doctors I had been attacked by a stranger. They didn't care, they never tried to call the police. They never tried to find the stranger who attacked me. I was just another black girl, who got what was coming to her," she said.

"Thank God I never saw Uncle Toot again until the day of his funeral."

JoAnn paused to wipe the tears from her face. "Things got quiet in my head. Something in me died. Gramps changed to. All he'd taught me - sit up straight, mind your manners, act like a lady. Smile. Be a good girl. All that didn't make sense no more."

Reneata sat and listened in agony. How could no one know? How could JoAnn and Gramps keep something so horrible a secret for so long?

She hurt for her mother, and she understood now why Jo Ann struggled to love her kids the way they needed to be loved. She also realized that her mother's sorrow had become her own. Uncle Toot had created a trail of pain that led to her, Ervin and Tess. Unknowingly, they were descendants of a shattered past – a generational curse – that needed to be broken.

Reneata now had no doubt that she was attacked at Savoy's.

"Why didn't Uncle Toot go to jail?" Reneata asked when the silence in the room became uncomfortable.

"Listen to you. Jail? Why didn't Byron go to jail? Why doesn't every sick, perverted bastard that hurts a child go to jail?" JoAnn ranted.

"So, you just went on?" Reneata asked, angry and confused.

"That's what we do. We go on. Your son is on drugs. Go on. Your uncle rapes you. Go on. You broke, and no one can help you. Find a way, to go on."

"What happened to me, momma? What happened?" Reneata cried.

"You were drunk. Had been drinking more after Ty left. He was keeping you good and happy, but the second he left, you started hanging out a lot. Gramps was trying to talk to you. Even Ervin was worried about you. He was getting clean. Jail had done good for him."

"I remember hanging out – just having fun - but my drinking wasn't that bad."

"Yea, it was. You were self-medicating. Everything had you down. It was just a matter of time, we all knew it, especially Ty. That's why he left ... to get things right so you two could get out of here," she said.

"You passed out in the bathroom of the club, and some girls left you in the stall on your face. Turned out the lights and told the club owner the bathroom was out of order. He put a sign on the door. Never checked if anybody was in there," she continued. "A while later, some guys got into the bathroom and found you. Whoever those girls were, they set you up. Them boys raped you." She stopped, took the back of her hand, and wiped tears from her face.

Reneata sat, listening in disbelief. How could so much have happened to her, and she didn't remember?

"It was pretty bad, but you were so drunk you didn't come

to until the clean-up crew found you. You were hurt. Bleeding. Sick to your stomach. They called the ambulance, but you wouldn't go. Instead, you called Ervin, and he came and got you. He brought you home. Got you in the shower. Cleaned you up and called me to come and sit with you. I stayed there overnight. You didn't say a word the whole time. You just sat on the side of the bed with your back to me, crying."

"Why don't I remember?" Reneata cried.

"The next day, you just went on as if nothing had happened. I watched you get dressed, put your make-up on, and go to work. The doctors had a name for it, but your memory of the incident wasn't there. The liquor, the stress, the shame... all played a part. You just didn't say anything. We asked about the bathroom, and you said nothing happened. You were obviously hurt, but you didn't want no help."

"I know when I think about the days leading up to Ervin's death, I don't remember much but the day Ty left. Nothing more," she cried.

"I know I changed after I left the hospital. I cried every time a man touched me until I met Cory. And even with him, I don't care much for sex."

"Your body was telling you something your mind wasn't ready to accept. I know. After Uncle Toot hurt me, I hated my body so much. I felt dirty all the time. I got my cycle for the first time shortly after that, and I thought something was wrong with me. I didn't have no momma around to tell me no different."

"You had Gramps."

"He was as broken as I was. He just let me go on as if nothing happened. I think he thought time would save me, make me forget. But it didn't. That's why, if you didn't remember, I thought it was the best for you, best for all of us."

"You thought time would make it right for me? Did it make it right for you?" Reneata asked angrily. "That was not what a momma should do. I needed something. I don't know what, but I needed something. You just went away and prayed everything would fix itself. Just like you did with Ervin and the drugs?"

"Wait!" she said angrily. "You good, right? Getting married to a half-decent man with a shit load of money? So, I was right. Staying away and letting you heal, worked. What could I do for you other than make it worse?"

"You got to ask that? You could have got me help. You could have told me what happened."

"We did! Why you think you stayed with Dr. Brown for so long?"

"All these years, I thought I was with Dr. Brown because of what happened to Ervin, and what I did to myself. I didn't want to live, and I had no idea why. It was easier, thinking my suicide attempt was about Ervin, but deep down I knew it was about something else. What happened the day he died? Just tell me."

"Ervin went looking for the guys that hurt you. He was staying away from drugs. Doing well, but he had a setback. He was angry, we all were. He wanted them boys dead. But when he hit the streets, looking for them, what he found was a dealer with everything he needed to get a fix. He fell off. We knew it was gone happen. But no one was more hurt by it then he was."

"Because of me, he had a setback?" Reneata cried.

"Don't see it that way. It wasn't your fault what happened to you," she said.

"It was my fault he lost his strength to stay off the street. Ty warned me to stay out the club."

"We were all warning you, but you were so hurt by so many things. Every decision since Byron. Giving up that baby when you were a baby yourself. Brad and that mess I got you into. Then Ervin, prison, and the drugs, we were all living a nightmare."

"You knew about the baby?" Reneata asked, surprised.

"Byron told me the night I went to see him about Ervin. Bragged about it. That boy thought he had your mind."

Reneata sat and cried for a while before JoAnn reached for her hand. Reluctantly, she grabbed it, and JoAnn pulled her into a loving embrace. The two women held each other until their tears no longer flowed.

"Cory knows?" JoAnn finally asked, when they were both seated back at the table.

"No. He doesn't know anything."

"That ain't a good way to start a marriage."

"I know."

"Why come back?"

"I couldn't bear the guilt no longer."

"No one is angry with you. We just trying to learn to heal."

"I thought, by being here, I would keep you from healing," Reneata confessed.

JoAnn took Reneata by the hands and looked her squarely in the eyes. "You are doing what I did - running away from the problem. But that's not the right way, trust me. I want you to be better than me. Don't let your past determine your future. Be braver than that. I have lost everything because I never wanted to deal with what Uncle Toot did to me. I had no idea that pain could travel so far but look at me, look at us. We are still saddled with Uncle Toot's failures. You can end this for yourself. And I promise to end this for you, me, and the family I have left."

Reneata grabbed JoAnn and held her in a tense embrace.

For the second time in her life, she could feel the throb of JoAnn's heartbeat against her chest, just like the day her mother fought to save her after the suicide attempt. But that day was long ago, and now they stood, heartbeat-to-heartbeat, bound no more by a painful past and family secrets. Instead, they were wrapped in a newfound love and understanding of each other that exemplified the unbreakable bond of mothers and daughters.

CHAPTER 26: GOODBYE ERVIN

Collier Billingsley Cemetery was cleaner than Reneata remembered. Money problems years before had left the grounds in shambles, until an investor from Huntsville stepped in to save what was once the most successful black-owned business in the city.

The investment paid off. The graveyard showed no signs of vandalism and lack of staff, as it had before she left Tinsley.

Ervin's grave was parallel to the third light pole at the highest point of the grounds. Reneata could almost pull her car right up to his headstone, which made her worry that, even in death, he wouldn't get much peace.

She found him easily, with Tess's turn-by-turn directions. Tess hadn't changed much over the years; she was still an avid reader and the guardian of all things academic. The fussy hair, men's clothes, and devotion to her new sexuality didn't change the girl Reneata helped to raise. Tess had still believed in doing what was right, even when no one else had. She stayed clear of the drama, when it came to Reneata and JoAnn's relationship. She intentionally stayed on neutral ground. No one burdened her with details of their misunderstandings and torrid secrets, they just assumed she didn't know, and was, therefore, safe.

Ervin would've turned thirty-nine that day. Reneata woke with his sixteenth birthday party on her mind. She had been too young to attend but she remembered her handsome brother running around the house, getting dressed, the generous coat of Old Spice he put on, and the smile he wore as he left the house. The party was at Gramps's place. Ervin's girlfriend during that time was Brandee, the daughter of one of the deacons at the church. She was tall, with creamy brown skin and long sandy-brown hair. She attended a school in the next town, but everyone knew her. State MVP in girls' basketball, and a 4.0 student, she was a legend in the old neighborhood because girls' basketball was as big to the community as varsity football was to every horse town in Texas. Ever since Demora Brownie became the first black State of Alabama girls' basketball MVP, straight out of C-Way, everyone followed the sport with an unexplainable fervor. It was Reneata's handsome and creative brother, Ervin, who was dating one of the most talented girls in the state.

By the time they were both sixteen-years old, they were in the newspaper, collectively, more than twenty-five times. Ervin, for winning every city and statewide creative art contest, and Brandee, for taking her team to the championship two years in a row.

Those were good memories for Reneata. Years before Ervin's addiction took a toll on the family, and a time when JoAnn was more at peace.

Reneata swept away the leaves and dirt that covered his headstone, before laying a dozen white roses on Ervin's grave. Ervin Lamar Littleton. A name that often-confused people who didn't grow up in homes where siblings had different last names, variant shades of brown skin, and noses that ranged from white man narrow to Marcus Garvey wide. In the sixth grade, Reneata punched TreSandra Gill in the face for telling her that Tess and Ervin weren't her 'real' sister and brother because they didn't have the same father. Their bond was as real as anything living and breathing that Reneata had ever seen before. It didn't matter if they were half-siblings.

From what Gramps told her, Ervin's dad was Turnip Littleton, a rookie police officer in the neighboring town, who was killed by a robber when Ervin was just a baby. Turnip was the only man who had wanted to marry JoAnn. Although he was twenty-four-years-old, and she was barely seventeen, he'd promised to put a ring on her finger the day of her eighteenth birthday. Unfortunately for all of them, he didn't live to see that day.

Some say Turnip was a skilled carpenter. Good with his hands, just like Ervin. But Reneata wouldn't know about that. JoAnn's discussion of him ended with the night of his death. She never said much about any of their fathers, other than what happened the day they left her. Reneata's dad walked out during a heated argument. JoAnn never said what it was about, but he never came back, never called, never thought of his little girl on her birthday or Christmas, or cared when she graduated from high school. Tess's dad stayed around for a while, but his wife wasn't happy about his girlfriend, so he had to decide between the two women. And since JoAnn was just some hood rat with too many babies, who had seen too many hard times, carved too many notches on her bedpost, and stood in too many food stamp lines, he chose to stay with his wife, who had known no other man but him.

Tess saw him often, for a while, until he got a good job in Maryland and moved away.

They were a pack of misfits. But what kept them grounded was the love of one man who never turned away from them. Gramps was the glue. He knew what they needed, and he worked to give it to them in his own way.

Reneata could not think of Ervin without remembering how loud he laughed. Hearing him in her head made her smile. It was the first time in six years she'd heard his voice so clearly. He was happy that she'd come to see him – she finally knew who had drawn her back home.

"You didn't forget," Gramps said as he placed his hand on her shoulder, gentle enough not to frighten Reneata.

"I was hoping to see you here." She turned to hug him.

"I'm here at least once a month. It's peaceful."

"It is. Where are you heading, all dressed up?" Reneata

asked, admiring his crisp white shirt and blue suit jacket.

"It's our fifth wedding anniversary. Me and Mill. We headed to dinner when I get back. You want to come?"

"Happy anniversary!" she said, giving him another hug. "I didn't know. But, no way. This is your day; I don't want to cramp your style."

"Our style?" he laughed. "You mean sitting in an expensive restaurant complaining about food we could cook better at home?"

"There you go," she said, and they both smiled.

Gramps took her hand, and they both kneeled over Ervin's grave and prayed. He started off by thanking God for his beautiful grandson and granddaughters. And by the end, they were both reciting the Lord's Prayer. Reneata had no idea she still remembered the words. It had been so long since she was in a church, but somehow Gramps knew she hadn't abandoned her faith.

After wishing Ervin a tearful 'Happy Birthday,' they both stood, hugged each other tightly, and started back toward their cars.

"Have a nice dinner, okay," Reneata said, just as she reached for the car door handle.

"Will do. What are you doing today? How are the wedding plans?" he asked, walking back towards her.

Taking a few steps to meet him, she stopped midway and stood with a confused look on her face.

"What's wrong, baby girl?" he asked.

"Nothing ... Everything," she finally admitted. The struggle in her mind, between telling the truth and continuing to hide, had been won by the latter earlier that week, after her talk with JoAnn. It had been enough. Everyone deserved to know the truth, especially those who sat for six years, wondering where she was and how she was coping. Standing there, steps away from the grave of the very person she felt guilty for not saving, and hearing his beautiful laughter in her head, she realized that his life was done; he was buried and now with God. What she had to focus on now was learning to live for herself.

"JoAnn. I mean momma, was raped by Uncle Toot. She told me," Reneata said.

"She told you that?" He pulled a white handkerchief from his pocket to wipe the sweat from his forehead.

"Is it true?"

Gramps took two steps toward her before stopping, wiping the sweat from his head again, then making a final move that placed him close enough to hug her. But Reneata stepped back, out of his reach. It wasn't that she didn't want to feel the safety of his embrace, but Gramps had always been a comforter for everyone. The problem was, at that moment, she realized that she didn't want him to comfort her. She wanted to come face-to-face with the truth, in a way she'd never done with her past. And now, with Cory, and a marriage that she wasn't sure she wanted.

Strength could be her enemy or her friend. But the strength she held onto had made her weaker because she had thought, to be strong, meant to move on without coping with reality. It was the real culprit her family fought against – maintaining a false sense of strength when they were too weak and fragile to handle the challenges life brought before them.

When Reneata stepped away, refusing to do what she'd wanted most for so many years – to ball her crumpled body and soul up in the arms of the one person whom she felt would always keep her safe – she knew it was time to come clean.

Gramps started talking before she could say another word. "Uncle Toot was a man, like so many of us during that time. We were taught to work hard for our families. But there was so much against us."

Gramps took out his handkerchief, folded it in half, and handed it to Reneata. She took it from him and placed it in her pocket.

"Back then, the freedoms your generation have, we didn't have. Black men couldn't do much in this city, in this state, but we still fought hard to have something. I worked thirty years in the coal mine, and everything I earned, I gave to JoAnn and you kids."

"I understand, but what did Uncle Toot do to momma?" Reneata said.

He reached for the handkerchief, but she refused to return it to him. It was, in some way, this unconscious peace offering between them that she no longer wanted to depend on.

"He hurt her. That's the truth. He hurt my little girl!" Gramps rubbed the side of his face with the palm of his open hand. Tears welled in his eyes.

"Why didn't you do anything?"

"Before me and Uncle Toot left Florida, we lived with my momma and her new husband in a shack on a dirt road south of Jacksonville. Her husband was a handyman who didn't work much, and she was sickly all the time. But she loved us, took good care of us before she remarried. When I was thirteen, and Toot was twelve, her husband got in trouble with the law and went to jail for a year. When he got out, he wasn't right in the head. He was borderline crazy, and me and Toot had to fight him off almost daily."

"But Gramps, what does this have to do with momma?"

"Uncle Toot got hurt by momma's husband. Hurt in a way I can't explain to you in detail, but he hurt him the same way Toot hurt JoAnn."

"But that doesn't excuse what he did," she insisted.

"No! It doesn't. But it's part of what made it hard for me to do more. Uncle Toot was a tortured man, he hated himself for what he did, and I made a decision I thought was right. I spared his life. But now I know, in sparing his life, I sacrificed yours."

"Momma needed help. She needed to deal with what he took from her," she said.

"That, and so many other reasons, are why I owe you kids my life. I should have better protected your momma."

When Gramps's face became soaked with tears, Reneata reached into her pocket and handed him the handkerchief. It no longer signified their surrender to the past but was a symbol of starting again, the right way.

"Life can't be about paying people back for our bad decisions – we all made them. It's not just you," she said.

"But your momma had everything going for her. I thought she was okay for a long time. She never talked about it, wouldn't let me talk about it after that sad ride home. She did good in school and seemed to be on the right track, until she got pregnant with Ervin. That's when everything changed."

"She was too young to be pregnant, but I wasn't going to leave her side. The day after she brought Ervin home, I saw a change in her. She wouldn't pick him up; she wouldn't feed him. Only when his daddy come by to see her would she put Ervin in her arms. When he left, she brought him to me and left the house. I didn't know what to think. But I was gon' be there for her."

"Did she ever get better?"

"No. JoAnn was crazy about you, but she couldn't connect. She treated you like a doll. Dressed you up all the time in pretty clothes, spared no expense on your things, but when it came time to do what mothers do … love and take care of your heart, she left that to me."

"Is that why Ervin got sick? Was he looking for love from her?"

"I don't know, baby girl. Nobody can predict these things. No one knows what happened."

"What about Uncle Toot? What happened to him?"

"I never went to see him again. I think about what he did to her every day. I should have called the law, I should have killed him, but I just remembered the nightmare that he went through, and I couldn't do it. I will carry this with me for the rest of my life."

"I feel so sorry for her. I feel like all the anger I've felt over the years was unfair. I thought she was incapable of loving us, but I was wrong."

"Hate me for it! Hate me, not JoAnn! She did the best she could."

"I don't want to hate anyone," Reneata cried.

Gramps pulled her to his arms, hugged her as tightly as he could. He didn't say a word. Nothing was left to be said. He kissed her on the forehead, returned to his car, and left the graveyard to make his dinner date with Mill. Reneata sat in the car for a while, staring at Ervin's grave and trying to understand how to navigate all the emotions she was left to sort through.

CHAPTER 27: MOVING ON

Making lists was something Reneata started doing when she was eight-years-old. She had a list of dolls she wanted. A list of books she would one day read, and a list of places she wanted to visit. She could make a list, but she rarely could follow through with a plan. Planning was a faith walk she was often too fearful to take.

That was why traveling meant so much to Gramps. He knew, if she could follow through – book the flight, find the hotel, enjoy her surroundings alone, the next step would be planning other life journeys. He was always one step ahead of her. That was why she loved him so much.

Hours after Reneata left the graveyard, she sat in the middle of Gramps's old bed, surrounded by torn out pieces of notebook paper. Each sheet had a list of things that represented what she knew to be true about her life, and what she wanted to be true about the future. There were words describing things she'd refused to acknowledge until that very moment, things that existed in the darkest places of her mind.

The Past: pain, loneliness, needing my mother's love, Byron, the baby, Ervin

Ty: love, commitment, safety, forgiveness

Cory: stability, new start...infidelity

Suicide Attempt: fear of acceptance, guilt

JoAnn had believed that black women could endure what black men could not. That what Uncle Toot did to her was what any weak and bruised soul would do if it could. That Byron, Brad, all her children's fathers, and the men who raped her daughter could only be expected to do so much. The bar was set low for them. Black women were the bearers of heartbreak and shame. They could survive any tragedy.

Reneata didn't want to believe any of it. She didn't want to be strong anymore. Instead, for the first time in her life, she wanted to be vulnerable, and for her heart to be protected. She wanted to feel the pain, learn to handle the enormity of it all, then work to move through it. She realized that her attempt to end her life had been caused by her own doubt that there was life after the pain she felt.

Sitting in the bed, thinking about what she'd lost, and what she had to move forward with, she began to understand something Bobby had once said to her, "Strength is the most misunderstood character trait that exists. People with a false sense of themselves define their ability to overcome hard times as an example of their strength and fortitude. But to overcome difficult situations, strength isn't the only thing that's required. Vulnerability and humility lead us to deal with, and accept, our circumstances so that we can change them and move forward."

All these years, JoAnn had hidden behind what she considered to be a black woman's strength. It had separated her from her kids. It had forced her to watch her son, who needed her to be vulnerable, destroy his life with drugs. It led her to miss out on taking care of her daughter when she was in the darkest time of her life. It was now the foundation for a life filled with cigarettes, liquor, dead-end relationships, and the loneliness of a soul struggling to deal with the past, accept her circumstances, and open her heart to those she truly loved.

This pain they bore wasn't started with Uncle Toot. It traced back further, to Gramps and Uncle Toot's stepfather. And maybe even further. How could she navigate her life off the winding roads of a generation of heartache?

Reneata refused to let JoAnn's story be her own.

CHAPTER 28: COMING CLEAN

"How's the wedding planning coming?" Cory asked.

"Honestly, things are not going as well as I had hoped," Reneata responded, rolling from the bed and situating the cell phone against her shoulder.

"What's wrong? Yesterday you said things were on track. I have over fifty friends and family traveling there in a few days. We need to get things going. What can I do?"

"Slow down, Cory. It's not the wedding," she said.

"Then what?"

"There are things we need to talk about."

"Ok."

After a short pause and a silent prayer, Reneata started talking, and this time she promised herself that she wouldn't stop until he knew the truth.

"I came here to reconnect with my family and my friends. But when I got here, I realized that reconnecting meant accepting my past. It meant finally dealing with what I left behind."

"Your past? What are you talking about? You're scaring me," he said, now in a tone that toggled between frustration and concern. "Is this about Ty?"

"Yes. Well, no," she admitted.

"Which is it?" he demanded.

"Listen. Please. Ty was the only thing about my past that I was honest about."

"Honest? What are you saying, Reneata?"

"My brother, for one. He was a drug addict and an ex-con who was murdered six years ago in my mother's house."

"Oh my God, Re! I don't know what to say. I'm sorry. Why didn't you tell me before? You said he died in a car accident."

"I did. It was what I wanted you to think. It was easier to say he died in a car accident than to admit the truth. I didn't think you would understand."

"I'm sorry you thought that, and I do understand," he sincerely replied.

"Thank you. But knowing about Ervin also meant that you would know the truth about my family. We aren't middle-class like I said. I grew up in public housing, never had much, and I was ashamed to tell you that."

"Did you think I would judge you? You were a kid who lived the life your parents provided for you. There's no shame in that," he said. "But why do I feel like this isn't about public housing or even drugs … what's going on?"

Another awkward silence occurred. "My brother, his name was Ervin, may have died because of my past. When I was younger, I got caught up with some bad people who sold drugs. I was a kid, but I was a part of it. What I didn't want you to know is I have carried a lot of guilt over what happened to Ervin, and after he died, something in me died, too. I tried to hurt myself, and I spent time away for it."

"Away? In prison! Were you in prison?"

"No. I was in a mental institution for several weeks after a suicide attempt."

The phone went silent. "Cory, are you there? Say something. I know this isn't the right way to tell you, over the phone and all. But things have happened here that I need to share with you before we marry."

"Ok," he finally said in a low and sullen voice.

"I don't know if I had anything to do with my brother's death, the police never caught the murderer. But what I did, caused a great deal of pain to my family and friends."

"You tried to hurt yourself? You never told me. I don't know how to take this. I don't know what to say."

"I was dealing with a lot. I was suppressing the pain from other bad things that had occurred in my life. I know that now. I can't explain it all. I can't make you understand the way I need you to. But it's a part of who I am. And if you marry me, you marry all that I am."

"How do I marry someone I don't know?" he said, as if he were asking himself, and never meaning for her to hear him.

"I can't answer that," she responded, just as the tears began to flow.

"We are getting married in four days. I don't know you. I don't know your family. I don't understand your life before me. Is Ty real? Do you have a younger sister? What am I to think?"

"You are to think about yourself. Don't think about anything but what Cory can handle, because the girl he loves is not the girl he met. That's the truth."

"Then who are you?"

"I'm Reneata Denise Morris. Tate is my mother's maiden name. I took it after I left the hospital and moved to Atlanta."

"What about school? When I met you, you were in school, right?"

"No. I was working at a strip club in the city. I was a part-time dancer, part-time bartender. The day we met; I had just left the club. I do have my associate degree. I was top of my class in high school, but I made a lot of bad mistakes. I drank too much for a long time, but I kicked the habit on my own. I'm ready to change my life."

"You lied to me for money! Is that what this is about?"

"No! I care about you. Please, believe me."

"Do you love *me*, or the idea of leaving behind what appears to be a troubled past? I mean, I'm not judging your life, your life choices, but you have left me with nothing but incomplete feelings and questions. What am I to do with this? Why are you telling me now?"

"I want you to either love me or hate me. Feel what you are feeling, and act based on your feelings. I haven't had that, ever. I've always done what was expected of me, by my mom, my granddad, or the guys I hooked up with. It's not fair to live a lie. I'm telling you because you deserve to know the truth, and I respect what you do with it."

After a short pause, and the sound of Cory's assistant entering the room, the phone went dead. Reneata tried calling back, for hours, but he didn't answer.

Seventy-two hours before the wedding, and Reneata was sitting on Gramps's front porch, sipping on a cup of hot tea and reading the newspaper. She'd lost hope that Cory would go through with the wedding after everything she'd told him, but he still hadn't called to officially cancel it.

She put the pastor and everyone else on notice that there might not be a ceremony. Tess was happy, and so was Ms. T. They both disliked Cory because they knew he'd cheated, and they were secretly hoping she would rekindle a relationship with Ty.

"You reading something good, or just pretending," Ty said as he walked up the porch steps.

Reneata placed the newspaper in her lap, then took a sip of tea as he stood over her, waiting for an invitation to sit down.

"What brought you by?" she asked while making room for

him on the porch swing.

"Just checking on you."

"Tell me you don't have time to check on an old girlfriend. What would the new girlfriend say?"

"She can't say much, since she doesn't exist."

"No girlfriend? That's right, you told me that. I guess I forgot," she smiled.

"Well, don't forget. That's a big part of what I need you to remember," he said, nudging her with his shoulder.

"Why is that?"

"Because, when you think of me, think of me as a man still looking for something special."

"Something or someone?" she asked.

"Someone," he replied, nudging her again.

"You know what? I've missed you over the years."

"You did," he smiled. "I wouldn't think...you never returned my calls, messages, or emails."

"You never emailed me," she laughed.

"O' right. I meant to, but I didn't have your email address or phone number once you moved to California."

"So, did you..." she said, leaning in to give him a nudge.

"So, what? Did I miss you?" he responded.

"Yea," she replied. "If that's not too much to ask."

"Come on, Re. I missed you so much I hurt on the inside."

Lowering her head towards the ground, she felt an unwanted sadness. "I'm sorry about that," she said without raising her head. "I'm sorry about ruining our plans, leaving here the way I did, and never looking back."

He gently placed his hand on her leg. "Don't apologize. You weren't ready. I know that now. And I don't mean because of what happened to Ervin. You were in crisis the first day I laid eyes on you stealing soda and a candy bar at the grocery store."

They both laughed.

"I was so young. I didn't know how to handle all the pressure I was facing. Maybe that's why I drank so much."

"Do you still drink?" he asked.

"No. Not even wine. I stopped a year ago. But I picked up other bad habits that I am working hard to fix. I didn't know I was so bad. I had no clue."

"I told you what a new start would do. I just wanted it to be with me," Ty said.

"What about you? You were supposed to see the world. How did you end up back here?"

"I did see the world. As much of it as I needed to, anyway. I spent a year in Korea, a year in Germany. I've been to Paris, Tokyo, Madrid. I also spent a year living in California, working for a company near San Diego."

"Wow. I thought. Well, you know. I thought you just came back here after the military. I had no clue."

"You thought I was doing nothing, like the rest of the brothers from the old neighborhood?"

Reneata, hesitantly, nodded her head. "I see I was wrong. What brought you home?"

"My mom got sick and she needed me. Plus, I was ready to get back to what I love - my pop's car repair shop. It's mine now. I turned it into a custom detail shop exclusively for luxury cars. It's doing pretty well."

"That was the plan," she said smiling.

"Yep. Got everything I said I wanted, but you," he smiled.

"I wish I could believe that," she said. "I wish I could believe that the person I was back then could have shared in your big adventure with you. Can I ask you something?"

"Anything."

"Did you know what happened to me at Savoy's?"

Ty turned his head in the opposite direction before looking her way. "Look, we don't have to talk about that."

"I know. I want to."

He took a deep breath before shaking his head, yes.

"What do you know?"

"I know two punk ass cowards took advantage of you."

"Hey, wait. Relax. I just thought, maybe, you knew something that can help me understand what happened."

"You don't remember?"

"No."

"I'm sorry," he said softly. "I know someone hurt you. Rumor was, it could have been Byron's brothers, but no one has seen those dudes in years, so I don't know how true it is."

"Wow. I hadn't thought of that. This just keeps getting worse," she said, turning away quickly to hide the tears welling up in her eyes.

"When I came home several weeks after the accident, everyone was talking about Ervin and what happened at the club. I called you a million times when I was away, but you wouldn't talk to me. When I got back, and you were gone, I went into hiding just to keep it all together. There was so much love for you and your family in the old neighborhood," he paused. "What happened at Savoy's stayed a secret for a long time, until Marco, the club owner, confided in one of the waitresses, and it got out. Believe me, there was no one who didn't want to find out who hurt you. Everyone understood why you did what you did."

"Really. No one said a word to me. I sat in the house for weeks before I left for Atlanta. No one said a word."

"How could we? You were locked away in Gramps's house, refusing to take any phone calls, refusing to see anybody. We had to accept that you had changed. We had to respect what you were going through, so no one said a word. It tore me up inside, but I had to go on as well, so I left for my first assignment in Alaska and I stopped trying to contact you."

"When I left the hospital, I was so ashamed. There was no way we could be together."

"Don't say that! Yes, it was," he insisted. "I'm not intimidated by your past. I know you. Sometimes I think I know you better than you know yourself."

"You do, do you? So, what will I do next?" she said, trying to force a smile.

"You will marry this guy, even if you don't love him. Because in your mind, you think he can make you happy."

"That's ridiculous," she said. "Who would do something like that?"

"You," he shot back. "That's who you are. You want happiness for others, but you've never had it for yourself. You would have done the same with me. Marry me when you weren't ready to, just to make me happy."

"I'm not that girl anymore, Ty," she assured him.

"Prove it," he insisted.

"Ok. How?"

"Don't marry him. Stay here. Grieve and learn to love yourself."

"Grieve? I've grieved enough," she said. "Plus, what's in it for you?"

"This isn't about me. That's what I've been trying to tell you. This is about the girl in the yellow sundress and flip-flops. This is about the girl whom I love so much that even after she shattered my heart into a million pieces, I still want to see her happy. With or without me. Learn to let people love you, Reneata. You deserve that."

Ty kissed her on the cheek, then left the house just as he had come ... quietly and sure of himself.

CHAPTER 29: BARE

Forty-eight hours before her wedding, Reneata hadn't spoken to the groom-to-be in days. If no word came by the morning, she would call the wedding off, catch a flight back to California to get her things, and try to start over again.

Ms. T. stopped by and brought dinner for her for the next few days. "Chile, no bride-to-be should be worrying about what to eat on the week of her wedding," she said, just before filling the freezer with plastic containers stuffed with greens, black-eyed peas, and smothered pork chops. Just in case that wasn't enough, she left a whole homemade apple cobbler on the stove.

That day was the only day Reneata sat in the house alone, from morning to night, watching television and nibbling at the crust of Ms. T's apple cobbler.

Ty called every other hour to check on her, and Gramps invited her to dinner. But she didn't want company; all she wanted was solitude.

It was 9:30 p.m., and she was showered and ready for bed. If no word came from Cory, she would be in Pastor Eugene's office at eight a.m. sharp the next morning. There was an afternoon flight to California she planned to make so she could have her things packed by the weekend.

Since returning home, she'd prayed every night, on her knees and without the sound of the television or radio in the background. Just her, the noisy crickets outside the window, and the sounds of the neighbor's front porch chimes in the distance. Tonight, was no different.

Halfway through the Lord's Prayer, she heard a knock on the door. Convinced it was Gramps bringing her leftovers from dinner, she walked to the door in her bathrobe and headscarf.

"Who is it?" she asked.

"It's me, Reneata."

"Cory?"

Surprised, she opened the door without hesitation.

"O' my God, you're here," she said, just before Cory kissed and hugged her tightly.

"I missed you."

"But you haven't returned any of my calls."

"I was angry," he said, while walking into the front room. Realizing that she couldn't disguise the tiny size of Gramps's front room and the poor living conditions of the remainder of the house, she felt ashamed and nervous.

"So, you're not angry anymore?" Reneata said, while walking behind him.

"Yes, but not angry enough to stop the wedding."

Reneata's eyes warmed. She gave him another hug.

"Did you miss me?"

"Of course, I missed you. It's just...I thought this was done."

"This? I don't understand."

"I told you on the phone who I am. My family isn't like yours."

"That's not important."

"It will be important to your mother."

"Well, she's not getting married, we are."

Just as Reneata turned to walk to the back to change clothes, he grabbed her and kissed her on the lips. She wiggled out of his grasp, then stumbled to the doorway of the kitchen.

"You lied to me, and I'm here, anyway, but you are treating me like I did something wrong."

"I'm just not trusting this. Why did you show up now? Where is your list of questions? Don't you want an apology?"

"I'll get to that in time. What list of questions? Is there more?"

"More? Yes, there's more. I'm learning more every day."

"Sit. Let's talk about it."

"Just like that?"

"Yes, Reneata. What are you afraid of?"

Instead of answering, she left the room to get dressed. While smearing on a coat of lip-gloss, she took a long look at the person in the mirror. This was her life, and for the first time, she realized that the image in the mirror was more than a lifeless doll. What awaited her was her future with a man who could give her everything she ever wanted. She had a big decision to make, but she had no idea how to make it.

"There's my girl," Cory said when she re-entered the room, wearing a pair of designer jeans and a fitted pink t-shirt. He had helped himself to his second piece of cobbler and a glass of milk.

Reneata sat at the table and watched him eat before listening to a thirty-minute recap of his day at work. He spoke as if nothing had happened. It was too surreal for her to comprehend. She wanted a loud argument. She wanted to try to either defend what she'd done or to find herself crying and begging him to stay. But that was never the relationship they shared. They had this calm and uneventful type of love.

After the pie was half-gone, and he was tired of talking about his day, they discussed the wedding plans and the honeymoon. His mother would be in town the following day to go over everything with them. She would need a security detail and a five-star hotel for a few of her colleagues. She would also be meeting with an old Yale classmate, a federal judge in the city she hadn't talked with in years, but who had the potential of being a big donor to her next campaign.

After hours of making calls to reserve hotel rooms, and unpacking Cory's things, he decided it was time for them to head to bed.

Once the lights were out, and they were lying body to body, Cory kissed Reneata's neck, whispered that he loved her, then climbed on top of her and started what would be a long night of lovemaking.

Afterward, he fell asleep immediately, while she lay in bed, listening to the rain and wiping away a single trail of tears running down her face. Cory did not notice the damp pillow or her shivering body.

She should have been happy, but she wasn't. With everything she'd learned, what would her life be like with Cory, back in California? She'd shredded a layer of her past; put it behind her, but she was still in the same place, trying to love a man who did not know the real Reneata, and who could not appreciate the growth she'd made or the long road ahead.

An hour passed, and Cory remained sound asleep. The rain was falling heavily, and thunder cracked the sky. Reneata quietly rolled out of bed, slid her keys off the table, grabbed her purse, and dashed from the house in her nightgown and robe.

When the car pulled into the driveway, she realized she wasn't wearing any shoes, and rain had soaked through her satin headscarf. She pulled the scarf from her head, let her hair down, and wrapped her robe tightly around her body before opening the car door.

Three knocks on the door were her limit. If no answer, she would get back in the car and go back to Cory. Two knocks down and one to go. Still no answer. One hard knock. Still no answer. She turned and walked down the steps in the pouring rain. But just as she reached the car door, she saw a light turn on in the front room.

"Reneata, is that you?" she heard Bobby say.

"Yes."

"Get out of the rain. Please, come in." He stood in the doorway as she entered the house. Soaked, she left a puddle of water on the hardwood floor.

"Wait here," he said, as he quickly left the room. When he returned, he was carrying a white towel, his robe, and slippers.

"Thank you," she said wearily. Standing in the middle of the room, she removed her wet gown and panties as Bobby watched. She could feel him staring at her naked body, but she didn't feel ashamed.

"Do you want some privacy?" he finally asked, but she was almost done.

"This is fine," she responded, her tone low and sad.

He took her wet clothes and placed them on the arm of a chair in the dining room.

"What are you doing here?" he asked, politely.

"I don't know," she confirmed.

"I don't understand. It's three o'clock in the morning and storming. You don't have any shoes on. What happened?"

When she looked at her feet, a rush of tears met a low and subtle moan of sadness. In seconds, she found herself on the floor, with her arms wrapped around the bend of her knee.

Bobby didn't move towards her. He just let her cry.

"Reneata, tell me what happened?" he asked again.

She took the lapel of the robe and pulled it tightly around

her body. For some reason, after allowing him to see her naked, she felt bare and ashamed.

"Cory came," she said. "We are to marry the day after tomorrow. But being with him isn't right."

"What do you mean?"

"For the first time, I felt everything. There were no veils to hide behind. There was just Cory and me."

Bobby extended his hand and helped her from the floor. He walked her to the couch, then sat on the coffee table in front of her. There they were, face-to-face, holding hands.

"Who was there before?" he asked.

In a daze, she tried to explain. "Reneata, the other one. The one living a million lies. Never wanting to feel the pain. Scared it would tear her apart."

"But who is this?"

"Reneata, the real one. The battered and bruised one. The one trying to pull herself from the ashes."

"What scared you?"

"Knowing that being real meant I couldn't go back. Accepting who I really am."

"What about Cory?"

"He loves me. Who would have come this far after hearing the truth?"

"But do you love him?"

"I think so," she said after a long pause. "I don't know. How do you know?"

"I can't answer that question for you."

"Why not?"

"I am not qualified to tell you how to love."

She gently released his hand and sat for a while, thinking about everything. Bobby left the room to make them a cup of hot tea and to put her clothes in the dryer. His house was so nice and peaceful. She wanted to feel ashamed for disturbing him, but she knew she had to leave Cory at that moment if she wanted to save herself.

"Drink this and make yourself comfortable."

"Thank you." She reached for the steaming hot cup. "Tell me something," she continued. "Why weren't you more shocked when I showed up?"

"I don't know," he admitted. "I just knew from the moment we met years ago that you and I would always need each other."

"What does that mean?"

"We have a special relationship. One that requires us to leave the door open at all times."

She shook her head, slowly, in agreement. He was right. There was no place she wanted to be more than with him at the moment.

An hour later, as Bobby caressed her shoulders and back, she fell asleep in his arms. He wrapped her in a warm blanket and let her sleep.

When his alarm clock sounded at fifteen past six, she jumped from the couch, found her clothes, and got dressed. Bobby watched, without saying a word. He had given her just what she needed.

"Come here," he said before she left the house.

"Love is a wonderful thing. I pray you have it with Cory, if that's what you want. But I am here if you need something else, something more."

He pulled her close, kissed her on the forehead, then

watched from the porch as she drove away.

CHAPTER 30: WEDDING DAY

The train of her wedding dress was close to six-feet long. Rows of white lace covered the figure-flattering gown, but the train itself was the most beautifully crafted coat of satin ever made. The fine trim of lace made it even more unforgettable. The day she found the dress, was the very day Cory asked her to marry him. She had walked into the dress shop on Rodeo Drive, the same one she'd visited weekly for months, and asked for the gown in the window. The very one, hundreds of wealthy women in LA had admired a million times.

The price was astronomical. But she had to have it, and trading an LA wedding for a Tinsley wedding gave her the budget to buy it.

She dressed alone. Her one bridesmaid, Tess, and JoAnn, whom she'd called and asked to stand with her as a maid of honor, were in a suite in the best hotel in the city, a gift from her and Cory. Full body massages, champagne, lobster, and diamond-studded earrings, compliments of Senator Debose. This day was what she'd dreamed of a million times. Here, in her hometown, in the church she was baptized in when she was ten-years-old. The very church Gramps stood in the doorway of every Sunday morning, welcoming congregants, before taking his place in the front pew with the other deacons.

Reneata sat in a tiny room in the rear of the church, listening to jazz music played softly on a small handheld radio. A beautiful statue of a white dove, that Ervin had created and donated to the church, sat in a display case near the door. Just knowing it was there made her feel he was with her.

She was dressed an hour before the wedding was to start. About every ten minutes, a friend or family member would poke their head into the room to check on her, but she wanted to be alone. She wanted to come to this day resolved that she – and she alone - had decided to wrap herself in a beautiful gown, apply her makeup, meet Gramps at the entrance of the main sanctuary, and walk down the aisle to her new husband. They were only moments away from starting their new life together.

Cory's mother arrived a day before the wedding. But Reneata hadn't seen her. Between meetings and interviews, his mother had barely seen either of them. When Reneata returned to the house after going to Bobby's place, Cory had already left. He called later to say he went back to the hotel to get ready for a conference call. He assumed she had awakened early and gone to pick up coffee.

She was a lucky girl. Twice in one lifetime, she could start over. Once, after she left the hospital, and now, again, on her wedding day. She gets to start free. No secrets, no lies. Cory knows everything about her, and he still wants to get married. She told him about Byron and Brad, the stripping and the assault. What she couldn't tell him about were the anxiety and uncertainty. Although, she was working hard to put that behind her.

She'd decided to let Bobby help her discover how to live a better life. Convinced she could beat down her demons and walk out of the darkness, with his help, they made a pact to talk often and to build a plan that would move her beyond the pain of her past, but she first had to face what happened to her at Savoy's nightclub.

The day before the wedding, she walked into Savoy's Place just before the happy hour crowd came in. Standing in the restroom, in the very place where she was told, the rape happened. Ty joined her. Holding her hand, but never saying a word. She remembered the countless nights she'd partied with her friends, gotten intoxicated, then stumbled out of the club doors. But standing there, in the warm and musty stall, she knew that something bad had happened. The sick feeling she'd experienced so many times in the past, rushed in like a freight train. What happened in that room caused her to attempt suicide. She'd buried the memories in her mind so deeply that she no longer knew how to find them.

"Can I come in?" she heard Ty ask through the shut door.

"What are you doing here at the church?" she said, startled.

"I wanted to wish you well."

After a long pause, she pulled him through the door, hoping no one saw him.

"What do you want, Ty? You shouldn't be here."

"You invited me, remember?"

"Oh, right. Well you shouldn't have come."

"So, it was a pity invite or a 'look how great my life is' invite?"

"Neither, crazy." They both laughed.

"You look amazing," he said, giving her a slow and deliberate scan from head to toe.

"Not so bad yourself. Are you getting married, or am I?" she said, and he chuckled.

"Just in case you decide not to become Mr. Cory Whoever, I got your back."

"Funny. But I'm committed to being Mrs. Whoever today."

"Oh well, I tried."

"What are you doing here?" she asked again.

"Seriously, I came to wish you well. It's not me, but I'm still happy for you."

"You've got to be the most selfless person I know. Why

would you wish me well, especially after how I hurt you?"

"You didn't hurt me. You were hurt. I just wanted to help you heal. I've never blamed you. You did nothing but love your family and try to be happy."

"Thank you," she said, just before wrapping her hands around his broad shoulders. "You are the one person I never wanted to hurt. You always wanted the best for me."

"You are welcome," he said, and they shared a smile that said more than words could express.

"The next time I see you, you and Mr. What's-his-name will be before the church and God. There's a sanctuary filled with people, excited to see you happy. Take that in. Today is your day."

When Ty left the room, Reneata sat in front of the mirror, putting the final touches on her make-up. The only man she ever thought she'd marry had just walked out the door. It was surreal. She didn't know how to feel, but she'd made up her mind – Cory was the one for her.

Everything in California was new and untarnished, but it wasn't home. People smiled because they had things that made them happy. All this time, she had envied them. She had run from her past, from the countless tarnished, yet beautiful, things that she had in a small town like Tinsley.

LA would be her second home; Tinsley would always have her heart.

Standing in front of the mirror for the last time, she wrapped her train around her arm, then headed for the door.

The hallway was empty, as she had requested.

Just as she walked past the large and elaborate pane window that looked out over the church's parking lot, she saw Ty standing across the street. He shook his head, as if to grant her permission to come, then raised his hand high enough for her to see it. The smile on his face was so sweet, she let out a long sigh, then covered her mouth to keep from crying. In his hand was a soda can and a candy bar - her beautiful lion had never left her. And in her heart, she had never left him.

Reneata stood in the window, watching him for a few seconds. She placed her hands on the window and thought of what it would be like to run to him and start again. But she could see through the small square window in the door leading to the sanctuary, that the guests were standing, waiting for her to make her grand entrance.

Gramps stood on the other side of the door, looking at Reneata with the sweetest smile. He knew not to open the door for her. She wanted to open it for herself. She wanted that final act to be her own.

The music played, but the door stayed shut. Reneata stood, looking at Gramps, and thanking God that she had returned home in time to share this day with him. She touched the window, and he touched her fingers through the glass. He had loved her whole.

Bobby stood in the very last pew. She remembered the countless times during her stay at the hospital when she had wanted him to kiss her. She now knew, with surety, that he not only loved her as a friend, but he also loved her for who she was, bare and uninhibited.

She knew, somewhere, standing in the front of the church were JoAnn and Tess, still healing from the pain that she was finally able to accept, pain that she had taken part in. But they were family, and together, they would get through it all.

The music played for longer than it should have, and the guests began to shuffle in confusion over Reneata's delay in opening the door. But Gramps, in his infinite wisdom, knew that by opening the door for her, she could not be true to herself. So, he smiled and waited and watched through the window.

When the song restarted, and she hadn't opened the door,

Gramps looked her way one final time. He saw in his grand-daughter's eyes what he could only see. He had never asked her whether she loved Cory, or if she was happy in her new life. Gramps just welcomed her home with open arms. He was there for her so she could heal.

When Reneata heard the pastor ask the guests to quiet down, she knew the time had come. She had to decide whether this new life and new name were enough to help her find her way out of the darkness. She had to decide if learning to love herself while learning to love Cory, was a risk she was willing and able to take.

When the door did not open, Gramps started walking towards the pulpit with a smile on his face. He knew Reneata – his beautiful granddaughter – his *Rambler* - was no longer waiting for the world to give her permission to be happy. She was gone again, but this time on an adventure to build a life for herself and to discover what true love is.

The End

RENEATA'S JOURNEY FROM DARKNESS TO NIGHT

Many people struggle daily with personal challenges such as poverty, incest, illiteracy, joblessness, fear, anxiety, mistrust, promiscuity and loneliness that may have had its foundation in their family lineage. Our ability or inability to overcome and move beyond these deep-rooted issues are often determined by our self-confidence and self-image and how we manage the stress, guilt and fear caused by the painful events of our past. Reneata and her family are examples of how one generations' refusal to face past indiscretions, seek help, forgive and move forward created the opportunity for these life-changing challenges to impact the physical and mental health, as well as the overall joy and happiness of their family. Unknowingly, they passed down from generation-to-generation the pain associated with living in poverty and the guilt of rape and incest because they were too afraid to accept and divulge secrets created by hurtful events. But what if building a roadmap from pain to promise, from helplessness to hope and from loneliness to love could be the start of healing hurting families and restoring trust and faith in our relationships? What if acknowledging the truth and taking responsibility for our role in the creation of pain could help derail how these experiences impact future generations? To help you imagine what this could look like, we have created a family tree designed to illustrate the legacy of pain and the promise of hope Reneata's journey entailed. The purpose of this exercise is to encourage readers to take a long and honest look at their lives and create a plan of action of their own.

PROMISE OF HOPE

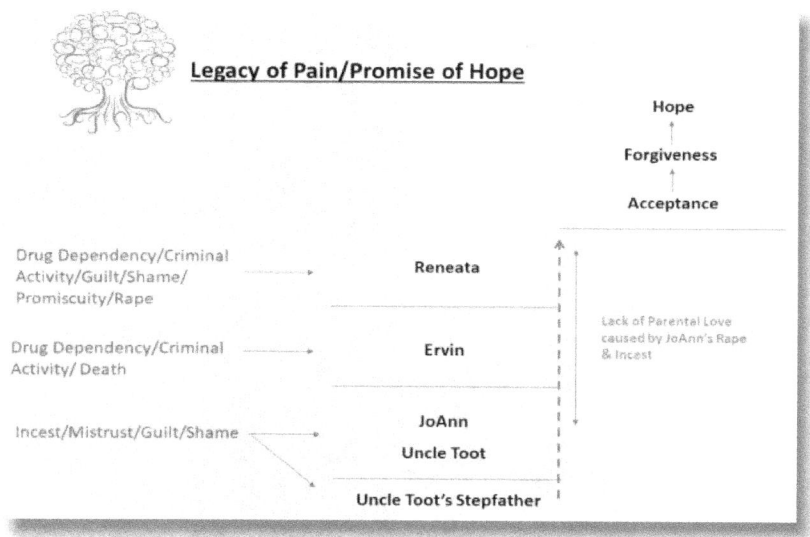

ABOUT THE AUTHOR

Michelle D. Jackson published her first novel, The Heart of a Man, in 2010. In 2014, she earned the second place award for The Authors Zone Annual Writer's Competition, General Fiction Category. She is also the recipient of the Princeton Literary Review Gold Standard.

To learn more about the author, visit:
www.authormichelledjackson.com/books

www.ingramcontent.com/pod-product-compliance
Lightning Source LLC
Chambersburg PA
CBHW060913180626
46817CB00004B/1243